PINE COVE

A SHORT STORY COLLECTION

HJ WELCH

SWEET SPOT

It's Halloween and Robin has prepared a sexy little surprise for his boyfriend Dair when he gets home from work. Hold on to your horses, Marine!

Sweet Spot is a follow up to Pine Cove #1: Safe Harbor and takes place after that book. 4.3K words.

ROBIN

"Wow, the apartment looks amazing." Robin Coal's best friend, Peyton, spun around, taking in all his Halloween decorations. "Maybe I'll stay in after all and make a night of it with you guys?"

"No!" Robin cried a little too loudly. He felt himself blush as he waved his hands. "*You* look amazing. The world deserves to see this incredible costume. Go enjoy your party. We're just going to have a quiet night in."

He fidgeted on the spot and tried not to look too guilty.

Peyton's grin suggested she was teasing about staying in. But she still looked surprised and gave him a twirl. "Aww, thanks, babe. I've been working on it for weeks. I have the hot glue burns on my fingers to prove it!" She wiggled her fingers at him and scrunched up her nose.

As much as Robin did admire her dark elf outfit, he was also aware that his boyfriend, Dair, was due home in the next half an hour. Peyton might be impressed with all the garlands and pumpkins and other spooky paraphernalia Robin had spent all afternoon setting up. However, he wasn't done yet.

He had to get *his* costume ready.

"This is kind of your work going away party as well, right?" Robin said, trying to sound casual. "Before we decamp to Pine Cove. You don't want to let your friends down."

Peyton hooted a laugh as she fixed her eyeliner in a compact mirror. "Okay, okay. I get the hint, lover boy. I'm going. Feel free to fuck anywhere except my room, all right?"

Robin spluttered in horror and outrage. "We're not-! I mean-!" At his feet, a certain fluffy puppy barked excitably too and ran around in a circle, chasing his tail. Robin pointed at Smudge indignantly. "We'd never do that in front of the children!"

Smudge was the only one dancing around their feet, complete with a cute vampire cape Robin had dressed him in. Jimmy the old bulldog was snoozing in his basket, unaware of the devil cape he was now wearing.

The three cats had hidden in case Robin got any bright ideas about dressing them up too. As if he'd dare.

Peyton laughed, gave him a hug, and patted his back. "I'm kidding. Sort of. Have fun. Love to you both."

With a wink, she grabbed her key and credit card to slip into her shorts pocket, then sauntered out the door.

For a moment, Robin remained where he was, trying to shake off his embarrassment. But what was he really shy about? He and Dair had been dating for five months. They were getting their own place when they got to Pine Cove. Of course Peyton (and anyone else) would assume they were having sex.

In fact, that was Robin's *exact* plan.

Nerves began to replace his humiliation. He rubbed his hands together and wandered into his bedroom with Smudge trotting along beside him.

A couple of months ago they'd just given in to the

inevitable and made Dair's room their bedroom and Robin's the one for storage before the move. He'd stashed the few things he'd ordered for his costume in one of the drawers here, in among their summer clothes. Their empty suitcases were stashed in the corner of the room, and on the bed were his koala stuffies collection, which Dair kept insisting on adding to.

Robin gave Smudge a pat on the head, then shooed him out the room. He felt like he needed a bit of privacy, even if it was just from their happy-go-lucky puppy.

One of the best things about getting together with Dair was how absolutely amazing he made Robin feel. Before, Robin had let his ex convince him he was no good in bed and nothing much to look at. But Dair...*god*, Dair made him feel like a fucking porn star. Robin had even been working out a little, loving the praise Dair had lavished on him for the slight increase in muscle tone. It wasn't that Robin felt he needed to look better. More that he was embracing celebrating his body with Dair.

And tonight, he wanted to show it off.

Was this completely stupid? Was it going to be mortifying? Was what he thought a special surprise for Dair actually Robin being self-absorbed and vain?

Was his choice of costume insensitive?

He bit his lip and laid the few things out on the bed that only guests occasionally slept in now. Slowly, he took a deep breath in. He was being silly. He knew Dair so well now. He wasn't this close with anyone aside from his twin brother, and that was a completely different kind of relationship. Robin had never been as vulnerable with anyone as he was with Dair. They bared their souls to each other.

Robin loved him more than *anything.*

And he deserved a naughty little treat.

Robin flung his clothes into the laundry hamper, then

himself in the shower, making sure he was fresh and clean in every possible way. Then he quickly dried, moisturized, and put in his contact lenses before shimmying his way into the tight little camouflage trunks he'd ordered. They really left nothing of his package to the imagination, and he fussed for a couple of minutes trying to arrange his junk so it was on display but also comfortable.

Then he draped the costume dog tags over his neck, fiddling with the pendants. What if Dair saw this as disrespectful? The Marines had been a huge part of his life. But he'd loved the little tanks and toy soldiers and other camo-patterned things Robin had bought him since they'd been dating.

Oh, for heaven's sake. It was okay not to be politically correct about everything, surely? He was just wearing a sexy costume for Halloween. Dair knew Robin would never devalue his service to their country.

With renewed determination, Robin did a shot of rum, then got out the stick of camouflage body paint. He drew stripes of the premixed greens, browns, and blacks on his face, his arms and legs, then finally his torso. Biting his lip, he checked his reflection meticulously in the mirror.

He couldn't help but think he looked cute. Sexy, even.

And now he just had to wait.

Dair was due home any minute, but now Robin wasn't sure where to wait. He busied himself with another rum, this one with a mixer. He wanted his wits about him, still. But he needed something to do with his hands and a task to preoccupy him for another minute. He kept glancing between the clock on the wall and the front door, stirring the drink with his pinky between sips.

What if Dair had gone out with friends for a spontaneous drink? What if he'd gone to the store? Robin had bought something simple for dinner if they wanted any later. Oh, god. What if Dair's day had been crappy and he just wanted to watch TV? What if-?

A key jingled in the door.

Robin shot up a very fast prayer that it wasn't Peyton forgetting something, practically dropped his drink tumbler on the kitchen counter, then dashed across to the apartment to drape himself against his and Dair's bedroom doorframe. He had less than a second to try and pose in a way that was seductive and not just awkward as fuck. So he popped his hip, laid his arm over his head so his fingers grazed his shoulder, and licked his lips so they'd glisten.

Of course, he'd totally forgotten about Dair's welcome committee. Jimmy and the cats had enough sense between them to stay where they were. Robin's behavior had obviously clued them in that this wasn't a normal night. But Smudge, the lunatic, ran up to his daddy with his little cape and barked his head off as usual.

"Oh, hello. Yes, yes, I know." Dair laughed as he bent down to ruffle Smudge's fur and allow himself to be licked. The door closed behind him and automatically locked. "Oh, look at you in your little costume! Aren't you adorable?"

That was to the dog, naturally. Dair still hadn't seen Robin.

He resisted every urge in his body to fidget, instead taking a long slow breath and keeping his eyes on his delectable boyfriend. Neatly trimmed blond hair, warm chocolate-brown eyes, over six foot tall, and muscles for days.

Robin forgot to be nervous and began feeling horny instead. How had he been so lucky to claim this man as his own?

"Aww, you're very excitable," Dair cooed, kicking off his shoes, his eyes still on the noisy Smudge. "Didn't Uncle Robin feed y-"

The word died in his throat as he finally looked up. Robin steeled himself as Dair's eyes went as wide as saucers and his jaw dropped. Robin took a breath, then looked at his man through his eyelashes.

"Marine," he purred.

Dair had been holding his gym bag. It landed with a heavy thud onto the floor. Smudge took that as his cue to leave, grumbling as he slunk off to his bed to chew on an old toy.

"Robin?" Dair took a step into the main body of the apartment, as if he couldn't believe his eyes.

Okay. This seemed to be going well. Robin's heart sped up but in a good, excited way.

"New recruit, reporting for duty, *sir.*"

He hissed the last word, then bit his lip. The way Dair was advancing on him almost spiked fear in his chest, although Robin knew he could trust his boyfriend with his life. But *fuck*, Dair looked like a panther or a lynx, stalking its prey.

As he got closer, Robin could smell the shower gel he'd used at the gym. A spicy, nutmeg scent. His blond hair was damp, and his eyes were almost black they were so blown.

"Hello, little koala," he rasped. Robin always protested that ridiculous pet name Dair had given him. But honestly, it was their special word, and that made it sexy. And in that moment, Robin wanted nothing more than to be cute and fluffy for his predator boyfriend.

He wanted to be devoured.

"Sir?" Robin squeaked as Dair discarded his jacket on the sofa, then walked over to loom over him. "I was told to report for orientation. They said a big, *tough* mechanic would take care of me."

Dair's tongue darted out over his lips. The lips Robin had kissed a thousand times and still craved more of. "It's that so, Private Coal? You seem a little lost."

Robin scraped his teeth against his lower lip. "I'm all

alone," he whispered breathlessly. "I was hoping you could help me, *sir*. I don't know what to do."

Dair was wearing sweatpants. So it was pretty easy to see the way they were tenting around his raging boner. Robin would never, *ever* get tired of knowing that was the effect he had on Dair Epping. This man could have anyone he wanted.

Yet he had chosen Robin.

Robin let Dair know how happy that made him on a regular basis, but it looked as if his message was getting through loud and clear tonight.

Dair chuckled, a dark sound that went straight to Robin's balls. Lovely, sweet, kind Dair, who adored when Robin talked dirty to him, and knew even more how exhilarated Robin felt to be so free with him sexually.

"I think you know *exactly* what to do, Private Coal," Dair growled. "I think you're being insubordinate."

Robin's breath hitched as Dair's knuckles grazed his hips on both sides. Robin's dick was throbbing in the tight trunks, hard and leaking a damp spot in the material. "No, sir," he said softly, his eyes on Dair's. But Dair's gaze was drinking in Robin's body with a kind of wild, reckless hunger. "I'm new and lost. I need someone to take charge. *Please.*"

Dair leaned in, nuzzling his nose through Robin's clean hair and taking a deep breath as he palmed Robin's cock through the satiny material of the trunks. Robin gasped but didn't move from his position against the doorframe.

"I think you need a little discipline," Dair murmured against his ear, licking the shell as he rubbed Robin's shaft. "As your superior officer, I insist you tell me what you want me to do to you. That's an order."

They both loved it when Robin begged for filthy things. He was already trembling, gripping onto the doorframe for support. "I want your big, fat cock," he rasped as Dair's lips trailed kisses across his throat.

Dair hummed. "Where do you want my cock, Private Coal? It's hard and wet for you. I don't know if you can handle it."

Robin whimpered and willed his knees not to buckle. His arm was starting to tingle where it was still draped over his head, but he wasn't moving just yet. "I can," he pleaded. "I want it in my mouth. I want you to paint my face with it."

Dair groaned, pressing his body against Robin's, running his calloused hand up Robin's side, then cupping his jaw. He leaned the other arm on the wall, towering over Robin, his mouth twitching with half a smile. "And how do you want me to make you come, little koala?"

Robin was quivering so much he was amazed he was still standing. "I want you to lay me down and jerk me off, slowly," he said, barely managing to get the words out. His face was aflame, and he squirmed. But as much as his breath was short and his heart was racing and his toes curled, he was *loving* this. Dair's dark eyes bore into him as he growled and leaned down.

"I'm going to fuck you, later," he said, his eyes sparkling with devilment. "Maybe tonight, maybe tomorrow morning. But at some point, I'm going to pin you down and slide my big cock into your gorgeous ass. I'll make it *so good*, baby. But if that's how you want to come first, I'll do that for you, gorgeous. Now, I think you should get on your knees."

Robin was panting as he finally moved his hands and placed them on Dair's chest, feeling his muscles through his tight tank. "Can I suck your cock?" he begged. "Is that an order?"

Dair came closer, touching his lips to Robin's trembling ones. "Yes, baby. You're so hot. Look at you. So pretty and all dressed up for me. You're so good. I want to watch you blow me. Take your time."

Robin chased his lips, grabbing his shirt as they kissed.

Dair's hands splayed across his back, his body pressing against Robin's and smearing his camo paint. He could feel Dair's cock stabbing his stomach as Robin humped himself against Dair's solid thigh. Breathless, he suddenly pulled away, dropping to his knees so fast it hurt, sending shocks through his body. He gave silent thanks for Dair's sweatpants, not having to bother with a zipper as he yanked them and his briefs down, exposing his big dick, rock hard, red and shiny with precum.

Robin moaned as he wrapped his fingers around the base and his lips over the hood, licking the slit with his tongue. There was a thud as Dair dropped his head back against the wall. They'd half made their way into the bedroom, so Dair shifted again and Robin angled his feet so he could push the door closed.

The last thing they wanted was a curious audience.

Dair had only just showered, presumably after the gym, but Robin could still detect his particular musk that drove him wild. His hard cock was hot in his mouth, and for a while Robin teased his lover with just his tongue and lips, stroking the shaft with one hand and gripping his leg with the other while Dair ran his fingers through Robin's hair.

The talking dirty thing was more Robin's kink. When Dair started coming undone like this, his murmurs became pure love and praise.

That still drove Robin wild.

"So good, baby," Dair whispered as he caressed the back of Robin's head and cupped his jaw. Robin looked up at him, seeing the adoration on his face. It made Robin's heart want to burst. "You feel amazing. Look so perfect. Don't stop."

Robin loved getting his boyfriend off with a blow job. He'd been so shy before they'd met, but nowadays he felt like he was in his element when he and Dair made love. Robin slid his other hand from Dair's thigh to stroke and caress his heavy balls. Then he sat up a little on his knees, giving him a better angle to swallow Dair's cock all the way down his throat. Dair grunted and banged his head against the wall.

"Fuck, *yes*," he hissed, pulling off his shirt and tank. "Just like that, sweetheart. I love it. Don't stop. Touch yourself, please."

His damn trunks were too tight. Robin hadn't anticipated this. But he was on a mission. So he sat up on his knees, his lips still firmly wrapped around Dair's cock, then using both his hands, he managed to shove his shorts over his erection and down his thighs. It meant he had to keep his knees closer together, but he could wrap one of his hands around his shaft, like Dair had wanted. With the other, he regripped the base of Dair's cock.

It was worth the effort to hear the filthy moan that escaped Dair's mouth as he looked down at Robin, taking in every inch of him.

"Perfect, perfect."

Robin bobbed his head faster, feeling the shaft rubbing down inside his throat. He reached up, stroking Dair's six-pack and pinching his nipple. Dair gasped and moaned, pushing deeper. Robin almost gagged, but he calmed himself, breathing through his nose and reminding himself he loved the sensation.

He loved even more how happy it made Dair. He began thrusting hard, fucking Robin's mouth, but never too rough to hurt him. They knew each other so well now, and that familiarity made Robin's heart sing.

"Baby, I'm going to come," Dair warned, grimacing and screwing up his eyes.

Robin risked a few more swallows, then came off Dair's magnificent cock to rub the tip on his lips as he started to blow his load. Robin closed his eyes as Dair's hot mess spurted over his mouth, cheeks, nose, and eyelids. Robin panted and squeezed his throbbing cock, not wanting to come himself yet. He just wanted to revel in Dair's pleasure for a moment.

He slowly blinked open his eyes as he heard and felt Dair dropping to the floor in front of him. He grasped either side of Robin's face, kissing the evidence of his climax. "You look good enough to eat," he murmured.

"Trick-or-treat," Robin said with a weak chuckle.

Dair hummed, kissing his lips deeply. "You're better than any candy, baby. Don't move."

Robin continued to breathe deeply, his eyes mostly shut as he sat on his heels, the trunks straining against his thighs, feeling dizzy with adrenaline. Dair must have kicked out of his clothes in record time because Robin felt like he only blinked before Dair was back, gloriously naked, holding a tissue to gently clean Robin's face and kiss any smears away that he missed.

"Tell me what you want now, beautiful," Dair said softly, running his fingers down Robin's arms. Robin loved that no matter what he begged for, Dair always checked again just in case he changed his mind. But Robin had discovered one of his favorite new kinks with his stunning boyfriend was them both watching him jerk Robin off.

That was his idea of a treat.

"Lay me down and touch me," Robin said, his voice hoarse from deep throating. He was trembling, feeling punch drunk and clumsy. He leaned his temple against Dair's shoulder, looking up at him. "Kiss me."

Dair nuzzled their noses together before capturing his mouth as Robin had asked. Then he used his impressive strength to slip his arms under Robin's knees and around his back and lifted him off the bedroom floor. Within seconds, the tiny trunks were peeled from his legs and dropped to the floor. Dair could then carefully lay Robin down totally naked on the bed, aside from the cheap dog tags that clinked.

Dair looped a finger through them and grinned. "You're too cute," he said warmly. "Did you get these from Party Town?"

"eBay," Robin admitted. He'd wilted a little and honestly wondered if he even needed to get off. He could probably drift into sleep right now. But then Dair spooned up beside him and ghosted his fingers along Robin's length, making him gasp.

"I love it," Dair murmured as they gazed through their eyelashes at each other. "You're my little new recruit. Private Koala Bear."

Robin snorted as Dair grinned at him. "Koalas aren't bears," Robin muttered against his lips.

"I know, sweetheart," Dair replied, his tone teasing.

That wasn't the only thing that was teasing.

He effortlessly reached into their nightstand for some lube with Robin hardly even noticing. But he was certainly aware when Dair's hand began to glide slowly but firmly along Robin's hard shaft. Robin groaned and buried his face against Dair's neck, his breath hitching. He was already so hard from all the buildup, but he didn't want to come too soon.

He wanted to make this last.

Dair whispered sweet nothings against his lips as they kissed, and Robin thrust his cock against Dair's hand. He felt so perfect. "Want you to make me come," he practically whined. "Only you. I'm all yours. No one else's."

He knew he was babbling, but he'd long stopped worrying if he was being embarrassing. After all the countless times they'd had sex, Dair had always loved whatever ridiculous nonsense came out of Robin's mouth, never once making him feel dumb. He smiled against Robin's lips.

"Is that so, gorgeous?"

Robin could feel his climax building despite having wanted to eek his orgasm out. He decided to just go with it. "Faster," he begged. "Jerk me off. Make me come. *Dair.* Watch me. *Please.*"

Dair increased his pace, pulling away to look Robin up and down as he twitched and shivered in the hold of Dair's strong arm, rutting himself against Dair's sculpted body. Robin felt totally exposed and yet completely safe.

That was the spell Dair had over him. Ultimately, it was always what pushed Robin over the edge, like it did in that moment.

He convulsed, jerking as he began spurting sticky cum over both over them, the little jets reaching impressively far as Robin gnashed his teeth and wailed. He clung to Dair's strong shoulders as Dair squeezed and eased the last drops from Robin's sensitive cock.

Robin gasped, his senses coming back to him as Dair leaned down and kissed his mouth tenderly. "Happy Halloween," Dair said with a grin, rubbing their noses together.

Robin laughed and dropped his head back against the pillow, high from his orgasm but also pretty exhausted. "Happy Halloween," he agreed. "Although next year, we'll have to work on your costume, Marine. Double D minus for effort." He pretended to pout while Dair dropped his head back and laughed.

"*Next* year, you won't know what's hit you. I can promise you that." Dair smiled warmly as he caressed along Robin's jaw, then down his neck and shoulder. "Next year we'll be all moved into our new place."

Robin's heart ached with love. Their very own home,

back in Pine Cove. Making their new life together. He smiled and nodded. "And you'll have twelve whole months to beat my costume."

Dair snorted. "There wasn't much to beat, sweetheart," he said with a laugh. "Literally. I might have to think of something involving body paint to achieve anything hotter."

Robin might have just come, but a wave of lust still washed over him as his mouth dropped open. "Oh, no," he said deadpan. "That sounds like a terrible idea."

Dair grinned as they began kissing, making out like teenagers. Robin loved how they could just waste hours kissing. It was his new favorite hobby.

"Speaking of terrible ideas," said Dair as they started getting a little chilly from the wet mess on their bodies. "How does dinner sound? Spicy chicken and greens, with some of those sweet potato fries?"

Robin smacked the back of his hand to his forehead. "Who will save me from such an awful fate?" he bemoaned. As much as he wanted dinner, they had been lying there a little while, and he could feel something getting hard against his hip as he rubbed against Dair's perfect, naked body. He sighed and looked mournfully up at Dair's amused face. "*Somebody* promised to fuck me. They said they were going to stick their huge cock up my tight little ass and make me come. If *somebody* really loved me, they'd find at least three different ways to pin me against this mattress and screw my brains out."

Dair's eyes sparkled as he grinned down at Robin. "Fuck, I really *do* love you, baby. *So* much."

As much as Robin was enjoying his dirty talk, he reveled as Dair touched their foreheads together, sighing as for a moment they just held each other, basking in their togetherness. Robin knew it wouldn't be long before they were fucking six ways from Sunday again. But what made it all the more special was the way his heart melted, overwhelmed with the knowledge that he was completely and utterly loved.

Halloween, Christmas, New Year's, Valentine's – it didn't matter the holiday.

He was pretty sure he and Dair were going to always love each other. And that was the biggest treat of all.

CROSSED PATHS

ABOUT THIS STORY

Raj Bhat is done living in the shadows. It's time for him to take charge of his own destiny and tell the man he's fallen for how he really feels.

Crossed Paths is a companion story set during Pine Cove #4: Bright Horizon and features secondary characters from that book. 6.4K words.

1

RAJ

This was a bad idea.

But then apparently most of Rajiv Bhat's life had been a bad idea.

Raj huffed as he left the family estate of Whittingar Abbey through the grand front entrance, using his foot to push the heavy door closed again behind him. Normally, he had to worry about his late great-aunt's Corgi making an escape, but today Raj knew the dog was otherwise occupied.

Everyone was, which made it the perfect opportunity for him to finally follow his heart and pluck up the courage to do the thing he'd been yearning to for months now. He wasn't going to be held back any longer. Not by himself, his snobbish family, nor anyone else. He'd recently been reminded that he was in charge of his own destiny, so it was about time he started acting like it.

Clutching a travel mug of tea in each hand, he winced as the cold November air hit the exposed skin of his face and hands. The light was dropping fast now that the clocks had gone back, but he could still make out the expansive English countryside that rolled away from all sides of the house. The orchards, stables, and woodland were to the right, which was where he was heading. There was no sense in dawdling now that he'd made his mind up.

He was facing his fears. Well, one of them anyway.

Unfortunately, making a decision didn't stop the nerves from fluttering in his belly like a flock of butterflies. He was no stranger to rejection in all aspects of his life from his family to relationships to his career. But the only person he was letting down if he stopped trying was himself. Deep down, no matter what anyone said, Raj believed he was a fighter.

So it was time to stand up for what he wanted. If he was rejected, at least he would have tried.

He bit his lip as he crunched over the long gravel driveway, heading toward the stables. The leafless apple trees rustled in the cold wind, which was also making him shiver. The tea was hot through the plastic travel mugs against his hands, though, and his determination was warming him from the inside.

More often than not, life might have taught Raj that when he tried something new or brave, he was going to get kicked down. But today had also reminded him that he wasn't alone. His sister, Anika, would never, ever abandon him. And if he was lucky, it looked like he had some new American friends on his side as well. Friends who had made clear to him that life was too short, so why not seize the day when you could?

It didn't matter if this was a bad idea. Because a *worse* idea would be continuing to drift through a life half-lived, and Raj was done hiding in the shadows. His heart demanded to step out into the sunshine.

His heart wanted Antoni.

Oh, gosh. Just thinking his name made Raj's heart skip a beat and his throat clamp up. But he inhaled a lungful of cold November air and tried to steady his nerves. "You're just going to say hello," he muttered to himself, his breath curling in smoky wisps around his head as he neared the stable. "No big deal. Apologize for being so shy that it probably came across as extremely rude, shake his hand, and…yeah…say hello. That's it. Easy peasy lemon squeezy."

He licked his lips and paused at the wide-open entrance to the stables, the rich smell of clean hay lingering on the warm air wafting from inside. Most of the horses were out in the fields with their coats on, so the stables felt oddly still and quiet. Golden sunlight stretched along the ground, as if lighting Raj's way. Try as he might, though, his feet now refused to move.

Raj didn't like the majority of his enormous family. As far he was concerned, they were stuck way back in the last century. Raj had allowed their old-fashioned ideals to stifle him throughout his childhood and adolescence. But why keep trying to please those people when they'd only ever tolerated him for being an 'outsider'? Why keep letting them shove him into a box he didn't belong in? He was never going to be straight, just as he was never going to be white. These were facts. But another 'fact' was that being gay in this family was the epitome of a bad idea.

He closed his eyes, focusing on the almost too-hot feeling of tea in his hands and biting cold on his face. He let the physical sensations to anchor him, calming his suddenly racing heart. There was no reason to panic. His many relatives didn't approve or accept him anyway. His great-uncle had already cut him off from any money he was owed, and the rest of the family wasn't interested in having a relationship with him. So what did he really have to lose?

Especially when he could potentially have so much to gain.

Keeping his eyes closed, he pictured Antoni Kolton clearly in his mind. It wasn't difficult to do. After all, Raj had been conjuring up his image ever since Antoni had started working for the family over the summer. Dark hair, shy smile, blue eyes. He'd become the highlight of Raj's trips here, making suffering though his family's usual jibes worth it.

In the past few months, Raj had visited Whittingar Abbey more and more to spend time with his great-aunt, Nancy, in her final days. She'd been one of the only relatives he'd truly ever felt love from, including his own parents. He blinked away bittersweet tears as he recalled the last time he'd seen her. She'd been weak, but she'd still had some fire in her as she'd caught him looking out the window, watching Antoni lead one of the horses across the grounds, rubbing her nose affectionately.

"You need to talk to that boy," Nancy had croaked. "Someone around here deserves to get lucky."

Raj laughed in the here and now, wiping his damp eyes with the sleeve of his coat. "Okay, Aunt Nancy. You win."

He managed to make his feet move over the hard ground, stepping into the warmth of the stable. The infrared lamps kept the workers and animals comfortable and toasty, and it was often where Antoni was to be found these days. He was employed as a groundsman. It seemed like he also threw his hand in with gardening, basic mechanics, stable groom, and any kind of heavy lifting task where his substantial muscles could be put to use.

Oh dear lord, those *muscles*.

Raj's mouth watered just thinking about the times he'd seen Antoni with his shirt off, working in the summer heat. Raj hadn't *intentionally* spied on Antoni while he'd been half-naked. But when he'd walked around the grounds like that, Raj couldn't help but stare.

It wasn't just that, however. Raj had experienced many (mostly underwhelming) hookups with gym rats while he'd been living and working in London. Unfortunately, most of the time they just wanted an exotic-looking twink to fuck and had left before the cum had even had a chance to cool. Raj had told himself over and over that he'd simply been grateful to find guys on Grindr without the infamous parenthesis *'No Asians'* firmly stamped at the bottom of their profiles. But the truth was, he wanted more.

He wanted kindness, which is what he hoped he saw in Antoni.

Raj felt like you could tell a lot about a person by how they treated those lesser than them. His ex-boyfriend had never thanked or even really looked at waiters when they'd gone out to dinner. It was not long after realizing this that Raj had dumped him. But Antoni was always respectful to everyone. When Raj had seen him murmuring gentle assurances to the horses as he brushed them, that was when he'd truly stolen Raj's heart.

In order to know for sure, though, Raj was going to have to stop clamping up anytime he was close to Antoni. Running away wasn't the answer, not anymore.

The fact was that Antoni might not be interested in Raj at all. Just because Raj had gotten a gay vibe from afar didn't mean he would be interested in Raj, especially after he'd been so standoffish. But all Raj could do now was try to see if there was a spark between them. If his attraction was one-sided, then at least he could be satisfied that he had stopped being rude. He would be *mortified* if Antoni mistook his aloofness as some sort of superiority complex like most of Raj's family had. They would barely even acknowledge the staff most of the time, let alone remember their names or speak to them. Raj wasn't like that.

If Antoni wasn't interested in friendship or anything more, at least Raj could do his best to persuade Antoni that he wasn't a snob. From what little Raj had seen, he liked

Antoni a *lot*. Anika kept telling him he needed to make more friends, so why not try and start now?

"Hello?" he called out as he wandered down the stable, anticipation rippling through him. Was anyone around?

He'd left Antoni here an hour or two ago, when he and his sister had unexpectedly been invited in by one of their new American friends. But Raj was ashamed to admit he'd once again been rendered mute when Antoni had spoken to him. The fact that Antoni continued to be friendly and polite despite Raj's terrible shyness gave him hope. Maybe Raj could start making amends as of right now.

If Antoni was still here. Just because this was where Raj and the others had left him didn't mean he'd still be hanging around. He was a busy man, after all. But Raj really hoped he wouldn't have to drum up his courage again. It had been touch and go whether he'd go through with the visit today. Who knew if he'd be able to convince himself to come back out here again? He had to hold on to this confidence while he still had it.

"Hello?" a voice called back from one of the end stalls.

Antoni.

Raj's heart leaped into his mouth, his feelings warring between happiness and dread. As much as he wanted to talk to Antoni, he had no idea what he was going to say and was even more fearful that Antoni wouldn't actually want to talk to him after all. Or that he'd feel *obliged* to talk to him.

Technically, Raj was Antoni's employer. Well, his family estate was. Raj didn't have anything to do with that. But he was aware of a potential power imbalance and didn't want Antoni to feel uncomfortable.

However, Raj couldn't seem to stop the way his hands were trembling at just hearing Antoni's voice.

Especially not when the man himself poked his head out from the stall on the left to see who'd called out. He was built like a rugby player under the gray hoodie he wore, with dirt streaked over his face where he'd been working all day. Raj had to suppress the image that flashed through his mind of dragging such a hunk into the shower to clean him off. Raj might have been shy, but he wasn't completely naive.

"Mr. Bhat," Antoni exclaimed happily, wiping his hands on a rag, then tossing it back into the stall. "Sorry, I mean Raj." He bit his lip as the brightness faded from his face. Was it Raj's imagination, or had he seemed pleased to discover it was Raj calling out his name? Then why had his demeanor fallen now?

Raj cleared his throat. "I-I'm sorry to bother you," he said from where he'd stopped several feet away.

"You're not bothering me," Antoni said quickly. He looked hopeful but didn't say anything more, and Raj didn't know what to do. It was like his mind had gone blank, leaving his body a quivering mess in the face of finally talking with his crush.

"Oh, um, good. That's good." Raj cringed internally. "Well, if you're not busy, I wanted to, uh, say hello. I mean, I know we've met several times before, but I'm a bit useless and always get shy. But then I realized you might think I was being rude, and I *definitely* don't want that. So, um, yes. This is me trying to be a bit less useless. Hello."

Smooth. Real smooth.

However, Antoni graced him with a warm smile. "I'm sure you're not useless." His voice was a low rumble that went straight to Raj's cock.

Down boy, he scolded himself.

Good. 'Not useless' was something Raj could work with. He took a tentative step forward, offering up what he was holding. "I thought you might like some tea," he said.

Antoni let out a little breath. "You didn't have to do that."

"I know," Raj said, trying not to let himself get embarrassed.

"I wanted to. I could just leave it here for you, if you'd like. Oh!" He balanced one of the travel cups on a stable door and fished in his coat pocket. "I didn't know if you took sugar?" He lifted up a small Ziploc bag of sugar cubes to show Antoni, as well as a spoon he'd taken from the kitchen to stir them in if necessary.

Antoni lifted his eyebrows…then he chuckled. The sound felt like it raised the temperature in the stable by a couple of degrees at least. Raj's heart skipped a beat, and he picked the tea back up before stepping closer once again. He held up the travel cup.

"Thank you," Antoni said, reaching to take the proffered drink. "And yes, two sugars. You're very kind." Raj felt like his heart was in his throat as he watched Antoni stir in the lumps, then took a sip. He sighed and wrapped his hands around the cup, fixing Raj with his beautiful eyes. This close, Raj could tell they were a stunning purply-blue, much like the wintery sky outside.

For a second, they just stared at each other until Raj felt heat creep up his neck. God, what the hell should he say? They had nothing in common. This was a terrible idea! He should just make a run for it. He should-

"Would you like to sit down?" Antoni offered suddenly, his expression excitable, like a puppy's. "I don't have any chairs out here, just bales of hay. But they're fresh and clean, I promise."

The words were out of Raj's mouth before he could stop them. "I don't mind getting a little dirty," he murmured.

There was a second where neither of them seemed to breathe. Then Antoni laughed with genuine mirth, dropping his head back, and Raj made himself relax a fraction. He'd not meant to make any innuendo, but seeing as he had, and Antoni had received it in good spirit, he took that as a good sign. He still might not swing for Raj's team, but chances were he wasn't outright homophobic, and that was a good place to start.

Raj followed Antoni into the horse-free stall that looked like it had just been cleaned and restocked. A rake was propped up against the wall, and there were several hooks with tack and other equestrian-related items hanging from them. Raj was ashamed to say he didn't know much about caring for horses. He'd barely ridden one despite practically growing up on this estate. His actress mother had always been too busy filming back in India to care for Raj and his sister, so Whittingar was more home to him than anywhere else, but he'd never really felt welcome there. Maybe that could change now?

The bales made a comfortable spot to sit on as Raj and Antoni sipped their tea. There was an infrared heater above them, keeping most of the cold away from outside, so at least Raj was cozy. Just when he was getting anxious, racking his brains for something to say, Antoni spoke up. But his words were surprising.

"I'm sorry," he said.

Raj blinked. "Why would *you* be sorry?" he blurted.

Antoni rubbed the back of his neck. "You said you felt shy. I was worried I've done something to make you nervous. I don't want you to be uncomfortable around me."

Raj managed a small smile, a tiny bit of his worry fading away. "Thank you. But it's nothing you did. It's just who I am. I'm nervous around everyone. Sometimes it can seem rude, so that's what *I* came out here to apologize for."

Antoni shook his head. "No apology necessary. I'm glad we could finally talk."

Finally? What did he mean by that? Excitement bubbled up inside of Raj. If Antoni had been hoping to talk to him as well, then maybe there was some interest on his part.

"How are you enjoying Whittingar?" Raj asked, scrambling around for the first question that came to mind.

Antoni nodded, also looking relieved for a conversation topic. "Oh, I love it, thank you. Very peaceful. Such wonderful animals. Your great-uncle is a good employer."

Shit. Raj would rather not have brought up the employee-employer relationship and especially not his miserable great-uncle. Raj would bet money that Kenneth was *not* a pleasant man to work for nor that he paid fair wages.

Awkwardness consumed Raj as he shifted on the bale of hay. This wasn't fair. Antoni probably saw him as an extension of Kenneth and felt obliged to talk to him, just like Raj had feared.

What exactly had he hoped might happen here? This guy was fucking gorgeous and hellishly masculine, to the point it made Raj ache all over from longing and desire. Why would he want to spend time with pathetic, weak little Raj?

He stood, feeling foolish, intending to make a run for it after all his grand promises to himself. "I-I'm glad you're happy here," he stammered. "I'll leave you in peace. Thank you for the chat."

He went to walk out of the stall, but a hand shot out and touched his own. Raj was suddenly very glad he hadn't bothered to wear gloves. He paused, looking down at Antoni still perched on the bales of hay, the air cloudy between them as they both breathed shallowly.

Raj's heart began to speed up.

"What *did* you come out here to say?" asked Antoni.

Raj shrugged. "I don't know, really," he admitted, "beyond apologizing for being rude. I just…I wanted to talk."

Antoni licked his lips. Fucking hell, they were plump and gorgeous. "Why?"

It seemed to Raj in that split second that he had two choices. Brush the whole thing off…or acknowledge the fact that Antoni's fingers were still loosely holding his own, and read into what that could possibly mean.

"Because you seem nice," he said breathlessly. "I was hoping we could maybe get to know each other better. I wanted to…"

Antoni's purple-blue eyes flickered as he took Raj in. "Wanted to what?"

Raj closed his eyes and inhaled deeply. "Stop watching from afar and wondering 'what if?'"

That was it. If he'd put his foot in it, he'd suffer the consequences. But this crush was getting too strong for someone he'd never even had a conversation with. Now he had, and he needed to know where the chips would fall.

Antoni closed his fingers properly around Raj's hand, causing Raj to gasp and open his eyes again. He watched as Antoni placed his travel mug down, plucked Raj's from his hand, then entwined those fingers as well. They looked into each other's eyes, and Raj hardly dared breathe.

"'What if' what?" Antoni asked, rubbing his thumbs against Raj's knuckles. His palms were calloused, but Raj loved the rough sensation against his soft and sensitive skin.

Antoni was opening a door for Raj, who was so used to seeing them slammed in his face. Raj was done wasting his time. He chose to walk through instead of running away for once.

"'What if' Antoni wanted to kiss me?" he whispered. "'What if' he didn't mind I had a stuck-up family, and wanted to take a chance on a simple, poor photographer? 'What if' he'd been as scared to talk to me as I had been to him?" He bit his lip, trying not to feel faint at his daring in uttering those words out loud. "Those sort of 'what-ifs.'"

For a second, Antoni just stared at Raj, giving him just enough time to question everything that had just tumbled out of his mouth.

Then Antoni tugged Raj's hands, and suddenly he was straddling Antoni's tree trunk thighs, with Antoni's large hands on Raj's hips under his coat.

Raj gulped.

"Hello?" he squeaked, as if they weren't rubbing groins but had instead bumped into each other unexpectedly in the park.

Antoni's mouth had popped open in a little 'o' shape, like he wasn't quite sure what he'd just done. "'What if' Raj wanted to sit on my lap?" he suggested with raised eyebrows, possibly unsure if he'd made a terrible mistake.

What he didn't realize was that now the shock was wearing off, Raj was positively melting from lust and excitement and pure relief. "H-he wanted that very much," he stammered, nodding and clearing his throat. "Uh, in fact, he's pretty sure he's very okay with anything you wanted to do right now…in the hay…with no one else around."

Half a smile tugged at Antoni's plush lips, his purple-blue eyes wide in apparent delight as they searched Raj's face. His fingers clung tightly to Raj's hip with one hand, but the other came up to gently caress the side of Raj's cheek with the backs of his fingers. Raj shivered deliciously.

"A quick tumble with the farm boy?" Antoni said teasingly.

That sobered up Raj immediately. He grabbed Antoni's hand and cradled it to his chest, feeling his eyes blazing as he stared down at Antoni. He looked surprised.

"I want the man I've been admiring from afar to share something with me up close and personal. But only if he wants to. There is zero obligation here."

Antoni blinked. "Right," he said, looking like he was processing Raj's words.

But Raj had meant them. He'd walk away this instant if Antoni was only doing this because he felt he had to. This wasn't his employer coming on to him and him not being able to back off. This was the accumulation of weeks of desire, building until Raj just had to know if there was any chance Antoni felt the same.

If he didn't, then Raj would leave that moment.

"No. There's no obligation on my part, I promise," Antoni said unsurely. "But you don't know me?" His brow crinkled in confusion, but when he looked up at Raj, he was positive there was hope dancing in his eyes.

Raj shook his head. "Not really. But I know you're kind and hard working. You care about the tiniest creatures. And, uh…" He knew he was blushing, even if Antoni couldn't see it on his brown skin. "You're seriously hot. I hope that's okay to say. I don't want to be a creep."

To his surprise, Antoni laughed. He moved his hand from Raj's hip to rub his back, sending electric sparks flying over his skin, even through his coat. "If it is, then we're both creeps. You're…uh…beautiful. I couldn't keep my eyes off you. But I didn't think you were interested."

Raj's heart was in his mouth, and his cock was finally daring to stir optimistically. This was really happening, and even though it was awkward, the reality was better than he ever could have imagined.

"It's occurring to me that there's been a lot of hesitation and doubt here," Raj said breathlessly. "How about we skip all that and just snog?"

"Oh, *fuck,*" Antoni groaned, his face barely an inch from Raj's. "I thought you'd never ask."

Their mouths crashed together as Raj flung his arms around Antoni's neck, climbing further onto his lap. Somehow, Antoni got Raj's coat off and pushed it to the ground. When his hands returned to Raj, he slipped them under his jumper to touch Raj's stomach and hips, making him squirm. Their kisses had quickly become frantic as they pawed at each other, rubbing their chests and stiffening cocks together. Even through both their jeans, Raj was excited by Antoni's firm length.

He wasn't usually the kind to leap into bed with someone, let alone start making out wildly in a semi-public place. But for once in his life, Raj felt perfect in his own skin. He was in the right place at the right time, and when Antoni called him beautiful, he believed it. He ignored the spiteful voice of his mother in the back of his head, telling him that Antoni was only interested because he thought Raj was rich. Raj had specifically mentioned that he wasn't. For *once,* he was going to believe that a man liked him just for who he was.

More than liked, so it seemed.

Raj gasped as Antoni stood, lifting Raj easily into the air with his legs wrapped around Antoni's waist. Antoni made him feel perfectly safe, though, with his sturdy hands splayed against Raj's back and under his arse. He kissed down Raj's throat as Raj moaned, then tipped him onto his back on top of the bale of hay.

Antoni crawled on all fours, looming over Raj as he breathed heavily, his hands resting on Antoni's chest. Raj could feel his solid pecs underneath the soft material of the hoodie. "I kind of want this off," Raj said, plucking at the toggles. "But it's too cold."

However, Antoni gave him a grin as he leaned back. In one quick motion, he tugged both his hoodie and the T-shirt underneath off, tossing them to the floor. His masculine musk from a day's manual labor wafted over Raj, making his toes curl with lust and need. Antoni's body was a dream, with deep grooves showing off his six-pack, bulging biceps, and those lines that led in a 'V' shape from his hips down beyond his jeans toward his groin.

Raj salivated.

However, it appeared he couldn't shut his damn mouth

up for two seconds. "You'll freeze!" he fretted despite his base needs trying to take over completely.

But Antoni laughed and dropped back down to hover above Raj. "Not if you keep me warm, beautiful." He groaned and slipped his hands under Raj's sweater again, finding his lips once more. "You have no idea how I've longed to pleasure you," he murmured between kisses.

Raj thought his eyes might actually roll back into his head. "Holy *fuck*," he rasped, digging his fingers into the hard, hot skin on Antoni's back. "Really?"

Antoni leaned away, pulling Raj so they were both sitting upright. Their noses brushed as they panted and looked at each other through their eyelashes. "You looked sad," Antoni said softly, cradling Raj's face. "I wanted to make you happy."

Raj nodded, stealing little kisses off Antoni's gorgeously plump lips. "I was. You are."

"Good." Antoni grinned and dropped his hands, yanking Raj's jumper over his head. Then he laid it on the hay before gently pushing Raj onto his back once more. "Because I'm very happy."

He rubbed his crotch with his hand and rolled his stomach, displaying the divine interconnecting muscles that rippled like waves on a pond. Raj definitely whimpered, his legs shaking and his mouth dry as he tried not to picture Antoni writhing like that against a pole. Fucking hell, he was *sinfully* hot.

Raj couldn't stop himself from reaching up and touching those firm abs with his fingers. Antoni bit his lip as he grinned, clearly enjoying putting on a show. And it was just for Raj, all of it. This sweet, quiet man had unleashed an exhibitionist from inside himself, because of Raj.

He couldn't quite believe it.

Raj knew he was slim and tall, but he wasn't ashamed of his body. He was still fairly fit and toned. So when Antoni bent down and began kissing his way down Raj's chest, he squirmed and enjoyed every second of it. The air on his bare skin was a strange mix of hot from the lamp and cold from the wintery breeze that cut through the stable. He could feel straws of hay poking his back through his jumper, the little pricks sending shocks through his body. All the unusual sensations were delicious and provocative as Antoni made his way closer and closer to Raj's straining cock.

"Is this okay?" Antoni asked, playing with the top of Raj's fly, checking if he could undo it. Raj nodded frantically, desperate for release.

"Very, *very*, okay. Oh god, please, Antoni. I want it, *yes.*"

He realized he was babbling, but he didn't care as Antoni made short work of his zipper. His erection sprung up, not constrained by the material of his loose-fitting boxers, and Antoni nuzzled it, mouthing it hungrily through the cotton. Raj groped at his thick brown hair, getting bits of hay in it.

He felt tears in the corners of his eyes as Antoni lifted the band of his underwear up, freeing Raj's cock. The air hit the damp tip, making Raj hiss at the sudden coolness. But then Antoni pushed the front of his jeans and boxers down enough to give him access, then slipped his hot mouth over the end and began sucking, and Raj didn't care about anything else.

He gasped and groaned, drinking in every second as he watched Antoni bob up and down on his throbbing dick. He used his hand to rub the base of the shaft, looking up at Raj with his sinful eyes like the winter sky.

If he was being honest, as much as Raj loved getting head, he normally closed his eyes while it was going on, losing himself in the pure sensation. But with Antoni, he couldn't take his gaze off him. After weeks of fantasizing, this was really happening. Raj wanted to be completely sure it wasn't some kind of dream.

Just as he was starting to feel his climax building, Antoni popped his mouth off, licking up the length like an ice-lolly. He kissed the tip, then wiped his mouth with the back of his hand before leaning back and unzipping his own fly.

Panting and trembling, Raj propped himself up on his elbows to watch Antoni free his long, thick cock. He stroked it a couple of times for Raj to see. "Want a taste?" he asked.

Raj nodded eagerly and made to scrambled forward. But Antoni gently pushed him onto his back again, then crawled up him to feed the big cock down Raj's throat and gently fuck his mouth.

Raj moaned, loving the taste of hot, hard, salty skin sliding over his tongue. He grabbed at Antoni's thighs and ass while Antoni caressed his fingers along his jaw and through his hair. "So beautiful," he murmured.

Raj would have been happy for him to come like that, but after what felt like only a few moments, Antoni pulled himself back. Raj almost complained, but then Antoni was kissing his mouth again, their naked chests rubbing against one another as their cocks bounced together. Antoni spit on his large, calloused hand, then captured both of their members so they slid against each other perfectly, their precum adding lubricant.

"Oh, god, *fuck*," Raj stammered, clinging on to Antoni like he was a life raft. Their kisses were quick and needy between panted breaths. Then Antoni buried his face against Raj's neck as he sped up his thrusts. Raj matched him, chasing his high as it started to build again. "I'm close!" he managed to utter.

Antoni nodded, not faltering. "Let go, beautiful," he rasped. Raj relaxed, letting his climax consume him. The orgasm hit like a steam train, and he jerked as he began spurting his load between their bodies. Antoni thrust a few more times before he joined Raj in his release. They shuddered as they came together, and Antoni cradled Raj to him, making him feel safe and protected.

It took a moment for Raj to come back to his senses. He gasped for air and blinked. The natural light had dropped significantly since he had entered the stable, and they were mostly just being illuminated by the glow of the infrared lamp.

He blinked and looked up at Antoni, suddenly afraid of what he might see. But Antoni's smile was warm as he laughed softly, brushing back Raj's hair and kissing him gently on the lips.

"Hold on a sec," he murmured. He cupped Raj's face to give him a firmer kiss before leaning back and stepping away from the bales of hay. He shook his T-shirt free from his hoodie, offering it to Raj so he could wipe off the worst of the mess. Antoni did likewise, then zipped his jeans back up before reaching for a blanket that was folded over a bar on the wall. "It's clean," he promised as Raj finished tucking himself away.

He realized with a jolt what Antoni was doing. He lay back down next to Raj on the hay, draping the blanket over them, then reached down for his hoodie to fold under their heads as a pillow.

They were snuggling.

Raj wasn't sure he was breathing properly. He hadn't known what to expect of this encounter, but cuddling afterward blew all his expectations out of the water.

"Are you okay?" Antoni asked, his expression searching as he let Raj rest the side of his head on his impressive bicep.

Raj blinked and shook himself, like he was pulling himself out of a daze. "Great," he said shakily. Then, fearing that was a terrible understatement, he stroked Antoni's chest and beamed at him. "That was incredible. You've knocked the stuffing out of me."

Antoni chuckled. "It was. I…I think I like you a lot, Raj. But I understand if I can't see you again."

Raj bristled. "Well, I wouldn't," he huffed. Then doubt seized him. "Oh, unless you'd be embarrassed?"

Antoni's laugh was so loud it made Raj jump. "Sorry, but that's ridiculous. Why would *I* be embarrassed, beautiful? Surely you'd be worried about being seen with a member of staff?"

Raj scoffed and scowled. "It's the twenty-first century. Besides, I'm not some lord. I'm a wannabe photographer. And also, I'm, uh…"

Antoni raised his eyebrows uncertainly at Raj's hesitation. "Very gorgeous?" he guessed.

That made Raj laugh, which he was grateful for. He hugged Antoni to him and gave himself a few seconds to find the right words. "I'm Indian," he said simply in the end.

"And I'm Polish," said Antoni, leaning back so they were face-to-face. "A lot of people back home would be ashamed to be seen with me."

Raj bit his lip and stroked the stubble on Antoni's face. "Those people are idiots," he said firmly.

Antoni laughed. "So is anyone who would think twice about being with you for something as ridiculous as the color of your skin." He found Raj's hand with his and brought it to his lips. "I'd like to tell you you're beautiful every day. But maybe we could start with dinner sometime?"

Raj felt the excitement leap in his chest. "Really? Like…on a date? Because there's this incredible Indian restaurant in town that I think you'd love. I know I'm supposed to say that British Indian food is nothing like real Indian food – and it isn't – but I still love it. Do you like Asian food?"

"I like all food," said Antoni with a wink. "But definitely Indian. It would be my pleasure to take you out."

Raj couldn't believe this was happening. He'd been

determined to be brave and reach out to the man he'd been growing ever fonder of from afar, but he never could have dreamed of a hot-as-hell tryst and then being asked out on a date.

They lay there in comfortable silence for a while, hugging each other and slowly coming down from the adrenaline rush. "What kind of photography do you do, out of interest?" Antoni asked just as Raj was reluctantly thinking he should check his phone and see what was happening with his sister and the Americans. Antoni's question caught him off guard a little.

"Uh, well, all kinds really. But lately I've been focusing on wedding photography." He smiled at his new lover. "There's something incredible about being a part of a couple's special day. I love seeing those happy ever afters."

Antoni beamed and brushed Raj's hair, making his skin tingle. "There needs to be more happy ever afters in the world."

"I couldn't agree more," said Raj, placing a sweet kiss on Antoni's lips.

There was a twinkle in Antoni's eye as he traced his fingertips up Raj's spine, then held him close. "Maybe there's even a happy ever after out there for us someday?"

It was cheesy, but Raj loved it. He laughed wholeheartedly and hugged Antoni tight. As much as his cynicism wanted to dismiss Antoni's words as folly, there was something inside him that begged to differ. Raj had never met a soul as gorgeous as Antoni Kolton's, he was sure.

Who was to say this wasn't the start of something long term?

Maybe even forever?

Raj mentally shook himself before he could get carried away. But as he snuggled with Antoni for just a little longer in their little slice of heaven, he figured it didn't hurt to imagine that he might have met The One. It happened to people every day, after all.

This was the right place and the right time. Raj Bhat felt at home in his own skin and in his gorgeous lover's arms. It might have been unlikely that a stable hand and the son of a Bollywood actress would have crossed paths, but the universe had obviously seen fit to bring them together.

Something that Raj considered to be a very *good* idea. And now he was going to do everything he could to make sure it stayed that way.

MIDNIGHT SKY

ABOUT THIS STORY

It's the night before New Year's Eve, and Taylan Demir is all alone, flat on his ass, and he's just lost his dog. Except when his ridiculously handsome customer, Hudson Perkins, comes to his rescue, Taylan doesn't just get his dog back. He's suddenly got a hot date, and maybe someone to kiss when the clock strikes midnight.

Midnight Sky is a stand-alone story featuring secondary characters from Pine Cove set between books #4: Bright Horizon and #5: Memory Lane. 11K words.

1

TAYLAN

Taylan Demir smiled at his final customer of the day as he walked him to the door of Turkish Delight. "That's very kind of you," Taylan said with a shy smile. "But New Year's isn't really my thing."

His customer, an exuberant guy by the name of Kamran, waved a finger at Taylan as he walked backward toward the door of the barbershop. "But New Year's isn't until *tomorrow*. This is just a few of us heading down to Aquarium. It'll be fun. Come on."

He waggled his eyebrows at Taylan, making him laugh. Taylan might have thought his customer was trying it on with him, but Kamran talked as fast as he drove. Flirting was like breathing to him. Taylan had to admit that it was nice to feel like someone was paying attention to him, but the thought of going to a crowded gay bar sounded awful.

Luckily, his rescue came in the form of a caramel-colored fluff ball that was scampering around his feet. "Thank you," he said with a soft laugh. "But someone is demanding her walk, and I have another busy day tomorrow."

Kamran opened the door to the barbershop, making the bell tinkle. A rush of cold air blew in. He arched a dark eyebrow and put his other hand in his leather jacket pocket. "You know you're not just our hairstylist, right?" he said, referring to his group of lovely but mostly coupled-up gay and bi friends. "You're a buddy. Promise me you'll at least think about the party at Sunny's diner tomorrow."

"Okay, I will," said Taylan, not sure if he really meant it, but not wanting to appear rude. Kamran and his friends *were* nice. But the idea of going to a party terrified him.

But the idea of yet another lonely night scared him even more.

He would try and think about it, he promised himself. In the meantime, he watched Kamran get into his dark blue Ford Mustang, which had been parked by the curb outside of Turkish Delight. He waved him goodbye through the shop window before Kamran revved the engine and sped off down the main street and out of sight.

Taylan sighed and looked down at his excitable Pomeranian dog, who he'd imaginatively named Pom. She snapped her head to look up at him, her tongue lolling out of her mouth as she panted.

"I'm not alone, am I?" he said as he reached down to pet the back of her head. "I've got my princess with me." Pom barked loudly and chased her tail, as if she was agreeing. Taylan chuckled. "Okay, then. Come on."

The other staff had cleared their stations before they'd left earlier in the evening. As usual, Taylan was the last one there, but seeing as it was his family's business, he took pride in that.

Probably a bit too much pride. He'd been so determined to make the barbershop a success after inheriting it when his father retired for health reasons he'd sort of forgotten how to look after himself. Sure, he still went to the gym and remembered to eat (most of the time). But his soul had been sorely neglected.

As he finished tidying and locked up, Taylan tried to remember the last time he'd gone on a date. Certainly not this past year. And he didn't do hookups with people he didn't know, so that was a hell of a dry spell.

New Year's was the night you were supposed to spend with that special someone. You were supposed to have someone important to kiss at midnight to signal the start of the new year. No wonder Taylan wasn't interested in partying with a crowd of couples. He'd be left standing there all alone when the clock chimed, facing another year of hard work and no one to come home to.

"Wow, I'm a cheerful guy tonight, aren't I, Pom?"

Taylan laughed ruefully at himself and shook his head as he and his girl headed down Pine Cove's boardwalk. He shivered against the breeze blowing off the lake at the end of the pier where the big fireworks display would take place tomorrow.

At least he'd be able to see that from his living room, and the thought cheered him a little. Pom miraculously didn't mind all the bangs and whistles too much, so as long as he kept the windows closed, he'd be able to watch the display and raise a glass. He'd be alone, but watching the town's display might help him feel connected with everyone else looking up at the sky at the same time.

Christmas lights twinkled and they swung from the streetlights like dazzling clusters of stars. The air was cold in his lungs as he weaved through the people out celebrating in town, a hundred conversations drifting over the wind along with music coming from several different places. New Year's might not be until tomorrow, but the town was still enjoying the few days left they had of the holidays.

When was Taylan going to start living his life? There was

a whole community here just waiting for him, but he'd fallen so out of practice with people it seemed too daunting to even try and start fitting socializing around work. He barely got time to walk Pom or to call his parents in California, often doing both tasks at once for efficiency.

But I don't want efficient anymore, he thought as he turned off the main street into the park. His apartment was above the barbershop, so he had a loop that took him and Pom around the streets and the small park that was perfect for cold, dark evenings like this.

Tugging his coat tighter around his neck, he smiled down at Pom as she proudly trotted along, her magnificent fluff dancing in the cold breeze.

Maybe the wind would blow him good fortune for the new year? Or maybe it was about time he took his destiny into his own hands and tried living a little differently next year. He'd spent so long throwing everything he had into Turkish Delight to make sure it didn't go under with him at the helm he wasn't sure what to do now it was a stable, growing business. He needed to channel that energy into building better relationships and stop saying 'no' all the time.

He wanted someone to look at him the way his sort-of-friends looked at their other halves. Like Robin and Dair. Emery and Scout. Hell, even Ben down at the baker's had gone and gotten engaged this Christmas. Taylan was never going to meet a nice guy if he didn't...

His train of thought was obliterated as his foot slid out from under him on a patch of ice. He cried out as he went flying up in the air, then came crashing down to the ground, slamming his butt and back onto the freezing path, completely knocking the wind out of him.

He wheezed and saw stars as he tried to catch his breath. Only then did he realize that he'd dropped the dog leash from his hand.

Pom was nowhere in sight.

"Pom!" he yelled in panic out into the darkness of the small park. He was between streetlamps and couldn't see anyone else. Fear flooded him as he pushed himself to sit up, his back protesting and his left hip throbbing. None of that mattered, though. Not when his little princess had vanished. "Pom!" he bellowed, then whistled, trying not to fear the worst. She was his everything. If anything happened to her…

"Hello? Is this your dog?"

Taylan snapped his head around from where he'd been peering desperately into the pitch blackness of the grassy park. A few snowflakes drifted through the lamplight as a man came strolling into view, a wriggling ball of caramel fluff in his arms.

Taylan sagged in relief, trying to swallow down the lump in his throat and blink back the tears that had almost started falling. Crisis averted. A kind stranger had scooped up his runaway pup.

Or…was he a stranger?

"I think she wanted to say hello." The man chuckled as he got closer. He was a little taller than Taylan, with honey-blond wavy hair, broad, muscular shoulders, and green eyes like a Christmas tree. Not that Taylan could particularly see all that in the gloom.

No. He had Hudson Perkins memorized by heart.

2

——————

HUDSON

Hudson Perkins had gotten more haircuts in the past six months than he'd had in the rest of his life. In fact, he'd hardly used his own razor since he'd moved back home. Why would he, when he could go to Turkish Delight and get a proper wet shave from the most gorgeous man in town?

He'd know Taylan's precious ball of fluff anywhere. So when she'd come running at him in the darkness, he hadn't hesitated to scoop her up in his arms to make sure she didn't scamper off anywhere else before they'd found her daddy.

Except, Daddy Taylan was on his ass on the icy pavement, wincing in pain and looking fraught as Hudson brought Pom back to him.

"Hey, dude," said Hudson as he jogged the last few steps and stuck his gloved hand out for Taylan to take. "You okay there?"

Taylan gave a breathy laugh as he allowed Hudson to help him back on his feet. "Sore, but I don't really care so long as Pom's okay. She ran off when I dropped her leash."

He tutted as he took the fluffy dog back and cradled her close to his chest. Even after falling flat on his ass, red-faced from the cold, with a bobble hat shoved over his glossy hair, he was still so stunning he took Hudson's breath away.

Maybe tonight would be the night?

Hudson bit his lip and watched Taylan fuss over his baby for a moment. When he wasn't flushed from falling over and panic, his tawny skin was usually smooth and glowing. Hudson had wondered many a time while he'd been getting his hair trimmed or beard shaved what it would be like to kiss that skin, and not just the bits he could see.

But no matter how many times he'd taken himself down to Turkish Delight, something had always stopped him from asking his crush out for a coffee. Taylan always appeared rushed off his feet, and it never felt like the right time to try and ask for a casual date. Hudson knew Taylan was single from chitchat they'd shared in the shop, but there was something about Taylan that always felt like he was holding back.

It was enough that Hudson had also held back every time, tipping extra instead of doing what he really wanted, which was to see what Taylan was like *outside* of work.

Now was apparently his opportunity.

"So, are you, um, done for the evening?" he asked.

Smooth. Real smooth.

Taylan shook himself and smiled at Hudson before placing Pom back down. His proper, big smiles were rare, so to see one now sent shivers down Hudson's spine.

"I am," Taylan said with a happy sigh. "Christmas and New Year's is always our busiest time of the year with people wanting to look their best for all the parties. But I have just one more day tomorrow, then a week off work. I can't wait." He suddenly looked concerned and waved his free hand at Hudson. "Not that I don't love what I do," he said hastily.

Hudson laughed and shook his head. "You're allowed to look forward to some time off," he assured him.

"Right," said Taylan, not really sounding convinced as he rolled his eyes.

Hudson wasn't deterred, however. He had the feeling that Taylan struggled to wind down. "Were you taking Pom for a walk before she tried her great escape?" It was pretty obvious that he must have been, but Hudson had to start a conversation somewhere.

Taylan laughed and looked down at his happy pup. She wagged her tail as Hudson looked at her too, laughing when she began to skip and dance at the attention.

"Yeah, before I fell on my ass," said Taylan. "I have this loop I do around the park and back to the shop."

"I thought you were done for the day?" Hudson asked with a frown.

Taylan shook his head. "I live in the apartment above," he explained. "It's a commute that I highly recommend."

Hudson laughed, feeling warm despite the chill in the air. They were slightly protected from the breeze off the lake by the trees around the park, but it was still pretty damn cold to be standing around.

"Would you like some company?" he asked, finally taking a chance to see if Taylan was interested in seeing him as more than a client.

Taylan's eyebrows went up. "On our walk?" he clarified. Hudson nodded, nerves fluttering in his belly. "Oh, uh, well, that would be lovely," Taylan stammered. "But don't you have plans? Were you going somewhere?"

Hudson shrugged. "I was going to head to Aquarium to see some friends. Well, technically my brother's friends, but they've adopted me. They're having a bit of a pre-New Year's thing. But I'm not really feeling it, to be honest."

Taylan frowned at him. "That's what my friends are doing. You don't mean Kamran and that lot, do you? The twins, Robin and Jay? Their friend, Emery?"

Hudson couldn't quite believe it. "Wow, yeah. My little brother is Micha. That's his gang who have taken me under their wing since I moved home. He's going to be there with his fiancé, Swift."

Taylan laughed and shook his head, looking disbelieving. "Wow, that's kind of crazy. I cut Swift's daughter's hair all the time. She's a dynamo." His face dropped a little, although he gave Hudson an attempt at a smile. "I don't want to keep you in that case."

But Hudson wasn't getting a 'fuck off' vibe. In fact, Taylan seemed really sad in that moment, and he hated that idea.

"Well, they're going to be there all night," he said with a shrug. "We could walk Pom, then maybe head over there together?"

Taylan bit his lip and looked torn. "It would be nice to have some company on the walk," he eventually blurted out. "But, uh, I'm not sure I feel up to a bar."

Hudson held up his hands and smiled. "I totally get you," he said with a laugh. "That place can get *rowdy*. Why don't we start with a walk and take it from there?"

Taylan blinked at him, and for a second Hudson considered taking the offer back and leaving the poor man alone. But then he seemed to relax and smiled, nodding as he turned to begin walking with Pom. "Thanks," he said, sounding a little breathless. "It's, um, nice to see you outside of the shop. How's work? Did you get that kitchen extension project finished?"

Hudson felt something warm unfurl in his chest as he fell into step with Taylan. Taylan was so good at remembering all the little things they talked about during their appointments. It made Hudson feel really listened to and appreciated. Not that he'd been neglected at all once he and his siblings had been adopted by their dads. But his family was big and unruly, and they always had some crazy shit going on. With

Taylan at the barbershop, it felt like a calm oasis where the rest of the world faded away.

Hudson knew Taylan probably did that for all his clients, but it didn't stop him from basking in the attention any less. He loved that Taylan remembered he'd come back to Pine Cove to run his own design and build company, and the nightmare he'd been having with that particular project.

"Yeah, it was a real bitch, but we made the deadline, just."

They laughed easily as Pom scampered along at their feet. Taylan was such effortless company. Hudson would much rather hang out with him than head to a noisy bar right now. It had been such a crazy busy holiday season. Yet another party didn't really seem appealing at all. Hudson would see all his friends tomorrow night, anyway.

A ridiculous idea started to form in his head, and he glanced over at Taylan. He'd seemed very happy to walk together. Maybe now was the time to be brave and ask him out to dinner?

He opened his mouth, but Taylan beat him to it.

"If you didn't want to go to the bar, maybe I could cook for you?"

Hudson blinked as he stared at Taylan. His light brown skin was blushing even more in the lamplight than it had before when he'd fallen over, and he bit his lip. The sight of that made Hudson's cock throb.

"You want to cook for me?" Hudson repeated. That sounded *much* better than trying to get a dinner reservation at this time of night.

"Sorry, that's probably stupid," Taylan rushed on. "It's just you said you weren't in the mood for the bar, and I was going to be cooking for myself anyway, but I'm making assumptions. It's a silly idea, just-"

"I'd *love* to," Hudson said firmly. He touched Taylan's arm to get him to look his way. He couldn't believe he'd been beaten to his own dinner proposal. His heart swelled. "Really. That sounds a million times better than another night of loud music and heavy boozing."

Taylan stared at him for a second, then that dazzling smile returned. "O-okay, then," he said. "Does spaghetti sound good?"

Hudson would have eaten peanut butter and jelly sandwiches if it meant finally getting a little time with sweet Taylan. "Sounds awesome," he said with a happy sigh, his breath condensing in the air in front of him. "Lead the way?"

Taylan smiled back at him, and Hudson noticed how thick his eyelashes were. They were so long they practically swept his cheekbones as he blinked. Hudson really, *really* wanted to press gentle kisses all over Taylan's lovely face. In fact, if he just leaned a little closer…

The moment was broken by a sudden string of Pom's barks as she yanked against her leash, straining to start a fight with…well, it could have been anything from a wolf lurking in the darkness to the softly drifting snow. Hudson did love how apparently unaware she was of her small stature, always willing to protect Taylan, no matter what.

He didn't really appreciate the interruption in that particular moment, he had to admit, but perhaps it wouldn't hurt for him to remember his manners. He wanted to be a perfect gentleman for Taylan.

"Yeah, uh, this way," Taylan said, pointing down the pathway. "It's not a long walk. We'll be in the warmth in no time."

Good.

Hudson was more than ready to have Taylan all to himself.

3

TAYLAN

FROM THE CURRENT PANIC AND CHAOS TAYLAN WAS
experiencing in the kitchen, anyone would be forgiven for
thinking he'd never cooked a meal in his life. "Sorry," he said
for the dozenth time to Hudson, who was propped up on a
stool at the breakfast bar. "This is taking longer than I
thought. The sauce isn't thickening, and I can't start the
spaghetti until-"

"Dude," said Hudson firmly. But he quirked a smile and
saluted the bottle of beer in his hand Taylan's way. "I'm
absolutely great, I swear. I've got a cold beer, good company
– by which I mean Pom," he added with a wink, then looked
down to where Pom was gazing adoringly at her new best
friend.

Taylan had to laugh, his nerves easing a little. "Of course,"
he said good-humoredly. "She makes a very good friend."

"The best," Hudson agreed. Then he licked his lips, the
neck of the bottle hovering dangerously close to his mouth.

Because that didn't look phallic at all.

"The chef's pretty cute, too," he said, his voice a low rasp
that sent electricity shooting straight to Taylan's balls. "I

bet dinner will be great, and I'm more than fine to wait for it."

"Oh, well, o-okay, then," Taylan stammered, trying not to blush.

But he couldn't escape the feeling that Hudson was flirting with him.

And not in the same way as Kamran, like he was just doing it to be friendly and pass the time. Hudson was talking to Taylan like he was the most important person in the world and looking at him like ice cream on a summer's day. It was a little hard to refute.

Which, Taylan tried to remind himself, *was a good thing.* He was trying to flirt with Hudson when he wasn't so nervous, after all. Surely the fact that Hudson had accepted his dinner invitation was a good sign, right?

Taylan almost spiraled into cursing his pasta sauce for not behaving on the *one* night it actually mattered. Then he mentally shook himself and recalled how Hudson had said only moments ago that it was all fine. The only person getting in Taylan's way here was Taylan.

"So, um, how's it being back in town?" he asked, changing the subject and getting the conversation flowing again. They'd been having a lovely time chatting back and forth until Taylan had begun stressing. He needed to stir the tomato-based sauce in any case, so he had to turn his back on his guest for a second, giving Taylan a moment's break to catch his breath. "Do you miss Seattle?"

"Not really," said Hudson, and Taylan glanced over his shoulder to see his expression anyway. So much for catching his breath. Seeing Hudson Perkins in his apartment was enough to make him dizzy. Taylan had tried extremely hard not to develop a crush on his client over the past few months, but he was only human.

"No?" he prompted, going back to his sauce.

Hudson hummed, sounding happy. "I mean, sure, I've got buddies out there that I go back and visit once a month. But I've been meaning to come home for a couple of years now. My twenties were kind of wild in the city, but I'm ready for a quieter pace again. I decided the time was right to take everything I'd learned and start my own business back home, near all my nieces and nephews. I've been too busy to miss anyone, to be honest."

"That's good. But the company is going well, yeah?" Taylan asked as he finally put the pasta in boiling water. He wasn't just being polite like he often had to be at work. He really wanted to know everything about Hudson's life. Taylan found him fascinating.

And that was almost certainly nothing to do with his golden skin, forest-green eyes, easy smile, or bulging muscles.

Nope. Nuh-uh.

"We're keeping above water," Hudson conceded. "It's tough to start up a company. We've had a lot of ups and downs, but I've got faith things will level out. I mean, what am I telling you for? You know what's it's like." He chuckled to himself, and Taylan turned properly back around, happy to let dinner bubble along for a minute.

"It's not really the same," Taylan said, shaking his head. "I inherited my business. You started yours from scratch."

Hudson blew a raspberry. "Dude, come on, I see how hard you work."

Taylan was ready to protest, but he knew full well he'd been obsessed with the shop ever since he'd taken the reins. "That's only because you're in there all the time, keeping me busy," he said, trying to joke. But the second the words left his mouth, panic flared that he'd been rude.

Except Hudson winked at him and bit his lip before sipping his beer. "Guilty," he said in that low rumbly voice of his. "But when you make me look so good, how can you blame me?"

Taylan's cock practically leaked in his jeans. Hudson *had* to see the bulge he was giving Taylan, right? This was really happening, and Taylan was done doubting it. "Well, you don't need much help to look good," he murmured, blushing but not really minding. "And I like you keeping me busy."

Hudson's mouth pulled in a scrumptious lopsided smile. "I see," he practically purred. "Well, maybe I could keep you even busier in the future, in that case?"

Of course that was when the pasta chose to boil over, and Taylan whirled around with a gasp, rescuing the pot and turning the heat down.

"Oh, shit," said Hudson with a laugh. His stool scraped over the apartment floor as he jumped to his feet. "Can I help? I'm distracting you. I'm sorry."

Taylan sighed in relief, having stopped the calamity for now. "Well, I do quite *like* being distracted by you," he said, sneaking a peek at Hudson from the corner of his eye. *Now* he felt like he was getting into the swing of things. "But I think we're almost done here. Maybe you could set the table?"

Hudson grinned at him and touched his elbow. It was such an innocent move, but it sent waves of lust rolling through Taylan all the same. "Sure thing," he said.

Within a few minutes, Taylan had the pasta dished up along with a salad he'd thrown together, and Hudson had managed to set out cutlery and napkins on the breakfast bar. Taylan didn't have a dining table, so that was the next best thing. Their only other option was sitting on the sofa with food in their laps. Taylan didn't mind that when he wanted to watch TV, but tonight, the bar felt perfect.

He grabbed his own barely touched bottle of beer and

took a seat. Although he was so excited he wasn't sure he was going to be able to eat a bite.

There was magic in the air.

So obviously, that was the moment that his mother called.

Taylan set his fork down with a clatter, the ringtone making him jump. Normally he welcomed a call from his mom. It'd been hard for him since his parents had moved away to a completely different state. But of all the nights for her to interrupt dinner, this wasn't the one.

"Oh, s-sorry," he stammered to Hudson as he retrieved the phone from his pocket. "It's my mom. I should take this." Pom danced at his feet. She loved doing FaceTime with Taylan's parents and their other three Pomeranians. But luckily, this was just a voice call.

Hudson shook his head. "It's fine. Go ahead."

"It's just that they're so far away, and I worry about my folks-"

Hudson squeezed his shoulder to stop him from talking. "Answer it before they hang up," he said firmly but with a kind smile. Taylan nodded bashfully and hit the call accept icon.

"Hi, Mom," he said cheerfully as he pressed the phone to his ear, throwing Hudson an apologetic look. "Sorry, I was just dishing dinner up. Is everything okay?"

"Oh, am I interrupting?" his mom replied, sounding concerned. "Nothing's wrong. I just wanted to say hello to my favorite son."

He rolled his eyes. She always said that, so he replied affectionately in the usual fashion. "I'm your *only* son."

"Yes, yes," she said with a smile in her voice. It sounded as if she was walking. She'd taken to evening strolls on the beach with her rambunctious fluffy pack, and Taylan thought he could hear barking in the distance and maybe the waves. "So, what's for dinner?"

"Uh, actually, Mom, I have company," Taylan said sheepishly, twiddling the pasta with his fork.

"Oh, you do?" she said eagerly. "Are you out with somebody? A friend?"

She sounded so hopeful, bless her heart. His parents had always tried their very best to be understanding ever since he'd come out in his early twenties. They didn't mind he was gay, despite what they themselves had been brought up to believe. They were just worried he was lonely.

But there was a good chance he wasn't going to be lonely tonight.

"Ah, no, not a friend. He's a client," said Taylan, glancing over at Hudson.

He didn't want to assume anything or get his mom's hopes up. But in that moment, Hudson slipped his hand over Taylan's knee and gave him a squeeze.

Taylan's cock practically jumped out of his jeans. That was *not* a casual or simply friendly touch. Their eyes met. Hudson shook his head, and Taylor's heart flipped.

"Sorry," he said, smiling bashfully back at Hudson. He was more apologizing to him than his mom. "I do mean a friend. I cooked for us, so I better-"

"You cooked!" his mom practically screeched in excitement.

Taylan winced and held the phone away from his ear. He'd hoped Hudson hadn't heard that, but from the way he was grinning behind his hand, Taylan guessed that ship had sailed.

"Oh, honey. I'm so excited for you," his mom gushed as he put the phone back to his ear. "Well, don't let me keep you. You boys have a lovely time. Oh! Make sure you be safe!"

"Bye, Mom!" Taylan practically yelled, hanging up before his mother could get any more embarrassing. He dropped

the phone with a clatter onto the breakfast bar and covered his flaming face with his hands.

"She seems nice," said Hudson, the mirth blatant in his voice.

Taylan peeked out between his fingers. "She's a menace," he protested. "I'm so sorry about that. I didn't invite you here because…well, I'm not expecting…"

Sex. Filthy, amazing sex with you, you gorgeous creature.

He snapped his fingers shut again and squeezed his eyes closed, begging the ground to open up and swallow him.

But Hudson's gentle touch startled him. Taylan opened his eyes again as his dinner guest eased Taylan's hands from his face. Hudson's smile was warm, and he rubbed his thumb over Taylan's knuckles soothingly.

"I came home with you," Hudson said, "because I like spending time with you, and there's only so many times I can go get a haircut or a shave. I've been wanting to ask you out for coffee for months."

Taylan gulped, hardly daring to blink. He'd been confident Hudson had been flirting with him tonight but… months? Really?

"Why didn't you?" Taylan whispered.

Hudson chuckled. The slow circles he was rubbing with his thumb against Taylan's skin were driving him crazy. His heart was racing, his breath shallow, and his dick throbbing.

"I wasn't sure you were interested," said Hudson. He licked his lips, looking at Taylan through his eyelashes.

"I-" Taylan's heart was caught in his throat.

Damn it. It had been so long since he'd dated, it was as if he was trying to use muscles he'd long forgotten about. All he felt like he'd done for the past decade was work. But what was the saying about riding a bike? Surely he'd remember how to do this if he just tried. Now was the time to be brave.

"Yes," he managed to say. "Yes, I'm interested."

Slowly, Hudson slid off the breakfast barstool. He moved between Taylan's legs, swinging the chair around so they were facing each other. Then he put his hands on either side of Taylan's face.

"Is this okay?" he rasped.

Taylan blinked, hardly daring to breathe. "Yes," he whispered.

Hudson's gaze swept up and down his face, lingering on Taylan's lips. "Can I kiss you?"

"Fuck, yes," Taylan pleaded, crashing his mouth onto Hudson's.

4

HUDSON

Taylan's lips were soft, but his passion was strong. He'd launched himself at Hudson, so the two of them were suddenly standing impossibly close between the barstools. Their bodies were pressed together as Taylan jammed his hands through Hudson's hair, pulling it a little. Hudson *loved* the short, sharp pain. It sent electricity straight to his balls.

Taylan's pasta might have smelled wonderful, but in that moment, the food was completely forgotten. Hudson kept one hand on Taylan's clean shaven, beautiful square jaw, urging their kiss deeper. The other he dropped to cup Taylan's ass through his jeans, eliciting a delicious moan from Taylan between their kissing mouths.

"Can I take you to bed?" Hudson murmured as he moved his hand upward, slipping it under the back of Taylan's sweater. His skin was warm and smooth, and he shuddered against Hudson's touch.

"Fuck, yes," Taylan uttered, pushing Hudson away from the breakfast bar. "This way, please."

Hudson couldn't help but snicker at Taylan's enthusiasm.

He'd always wondered if under all that shy politeness, there was a wildcat waiting to be let loose.

And here he was. He'd been worth waiting for.

Taylan had given Hudson a short tour of his apartment when they'd first come in. It was a pretty simple one-bedroom place with an open-plan kitchen and living room, so Hudson didn't exactly need a map to get to their destination. But when they reached the bedroom door, a small fluffy someone tried to trip them up.

"Pom!" Taylan cried in dismay as the two men crashed into the doorframe. Hudson clung on to Taylan's waist, keeping them both upright and close. Hot damn, Taylan felt perfect pressed up against him like this.

Hudson snorted as the small dog bounced around and barked, clearly thinking her daddy was playing a fun game with his new friend.

Well, thought Hudson, *we* are *going to play a fun game. It's just not a game for doggies.*

"Go on, off you go," Taylan said sweetly, shooing Pom back as he and Hudson edged inside the door into the darkened room. "We'll come back later. I promise."

Hudson chuckled and kissed Taylan's neck. "You're adorable," he said fondly against his skin.

Taylan huffed as he finally managed to back them into his room and close the door on his forlorn-looking pup. "I'm getting cockblocked by a ball of fluff on four legs," he grumbled.

But Hudson seized either side of Taylan's head and caught his lower lip between his teeth, watching it release before he bore his gaze into Taylan's eyes. "I can assure you," he growled. "You're not getting cockblocked."

"What am I getting?" Taylan asked breathlessly, flicking an eyebrow.

Hudson hummed. He hadn't been expecting Taylan to have a playful side. He fucking loved it.

"Whatever you want, beautiful," he said.

Taylan looped his fingers over the edge of Hudson's jeans to pull him toward the bed. He bit his lip and gave Hudson a sultry look as their legs bumped against the side of the mattress. Hudson watched as Taylan ran his hand up the sides of Hudson's chest. "You," Taylan said softly. "I just want you."

Hudson slid his hands under Taylan's thighs and made him yelp by picking him up. In a flash, Taylan had his arms and legs wrapped around Hudson as they kissed. Hudson could feel Taylan's hard length pressed against his stomach.

He wanted to get it in his mouth.

"You've got me," Hudson promised him, their mouths crashing together once again.

Taylan rewarded him with another delightful yelp as they toppled on top of the bed, their limbs tangling together as they rolled over the soft cotton sheets that were stretched over the enormous king-sized bed.

"This thing is half the size of my apartment," Hudson said, pausing to tease Taylan as he looked over the bed incredulously. "This is definitely a bed made for two. Have you been in here all by yourself?"

Taylan nodded bashfully. "All year," he admitted shyly.

Hudson nibbled at Taylan's earlobe, making him squirm. "Well, I'm very happy to help you with that."

"What excellent customer service," Taylan said, his playfulness coming back.

Hudson rewarded him with a kiss. "I learned from the best at Turkish Delight. Can I help you out of these wet clothes, sir?" putting on his best phone voice. Of course Taylan had dried off since he'd fallen over in the park, but it amused Hudson to keep going with the customer service shtick. He felt like a very naughty bellhop in that moment.

Apparently, he wasn't the only one enjoying the little game. "Hmm, if you do, I'll give you a good tip," Taylan purred.

Hudson kissed him filthily and palmed between his legs, feeling the hardness that was waiting for him. "This tip?" he asked hopefully.

Taylan dissolved into giggles, unable to keep a straight face with the role playing. "That's the one," he said happily.

Hudson would rather see Taylan smiling and free like he was in that moment than keeping up with some silly game. From what Hudson had seen in the barbershop, Taylan worked so hard and put everyone's happiness before his own.

It was time for someone to take care of him for a change.

He took his time undressing Taylan, kissing all that gorgeous skin as it became available to him. He sucked his nipples, licked down to his belly button, and pressed his lips to the sensitive insides of his thighs. Once Taylan was down to just his underwear, Hudson mouthed his hard, straining cock through the cotton of his briefs. Taylan gasped and bunched his hands around the duvet, but he was doing his best not to move too much, allowing Hudson to explore at his leisure.

Taylan smelled amazing. Musky and spicy like the products he offered customers at Turkish Delight. His thighs were warm, but his knees were cold. His feet were ticklish, and his belly was soft below his abs. Hudson mapped out his lover's body until Taylan was a quivering wreck.

He was about to whip off the briefs when Taylan began pawing urgently at Hudson's open shirt, trying to push it off his shoulders. "Now you," Taylan pleaded, plucking at the T-shirt underneath the flannel as well. "I've been dreaming about your body."

Hudson groaned, lust rolling through him. "Yes, sir," he purred, stripping his top half in a matter of seconds.

Taylan gasped as he ran his hands over his ripped muscles. Hudson didn't like to think he was vain, but he did work out a fair bit on top of his physically demanding job. He liked seeing appreciation on a guy's face in the bedroom, but from Taylan, it meant *so* much more. His heart fluttered, and heat rushed through him under Taylan's wide-eyed gaze. This had been a long time coming for both of them, so it seemed.

Hudson ground down on top of Taylan, kissing him with fervor and loving how their warm skin felt so good rubbing together. A thousand little sparks flared between them, rushing over their bodies. Even through his jeans, Hudson's cock was already having a *very* good time.

"Oh my god," Taylan gasped, breaking the kiss as he came up for air. He scratched his hands down Hudson's bare back. "I'm so glad I fell on that ice."

Hudson chuckled and nuzzled his neck again, pressing kisses along his pulse point. "Me, too. I just hope your ass isn't too sore where you hit the deck."

Taylan snorted and thrust his cock against Hudson's thigh. "I hope it's going to be *much* sorer come morning," he said, waggling his eyebrows and making Hudson throw back his head and laugh. "Would you like to top me?"

Hudson sighed and kissed Taylan's lips sweetly. "That's the most adorable proposition for sex I've ever had," he growled affectionately, nuzzling their noses together.

Taylan tutted. "All right, would you please fuck me hard up the ass, just the way I've been fantasizing about? I want to feel you all day tomorrow to prove this really happened."

Hudson exhaled. "Whoa. Okay, then, sir," he said,

grinning. "The customer's always right, after all. But I feel I have to assure you that this is *definitely* happening. No more daydreaming. I'm here to make your fantasies come true."

Taylan screwed up his eyes and dropped his head back into the pillow as he moaned. "Yes, please, yes."

"I hate to sound like your mom," Hudson said, chuckling as Taylan's eyes flew open in horror at the mention of his mother. "But *do* you have protection?"

"Oh, yes, absolutely." Taylan gestured wildly toward his nightstand. "Top drawer. Condoms and lube. All still in date, I checked."

Hudson laughed as he yanked the drawer open. There were all kinds of things in there, like a passport, notebooks, a few packets of everyday meds, and even some dog treats. Not naughty things, but still intimate parts of Taylan's life that Hudson was thrilled to see.

But all he was *really* interested in for the moment was the box of condoms and tube of lubricant near the top of the jumbled things. He snatched them up and closed the drawer.

As promised, they were all still in date.

"Such outstanding customer service," he joked as he jumped up and unbuttoned his jeans. He shoved them and his briefs down in one quick motion, kicking them and his socks away. "I'll be sure to leave an enthusiastic review online."

Taylan snorted and covered his face. "We haven't even fucked yet," he protested. "What if it's crap?"

Hudson peeled his lover's briefs down his slender legs, tossing them away. Now they were gloriously naked, he lowered himself back down on top of Taylan, covering him with his weight. Their cocks bumped together, and Taylan whimpered as he dropped his hands from his face, digging his fingers into Hudson's back.

"Oh, baby," Hudson said as he rolled his hips. "I already know this is going to be spectacular."

Taylan just nodded. It looked like words were failing him, so instead, he kissed Hudson demandingly. "Can I suck you?" he managed to utter.

Hudson hummed. "Well, *I* wanted to suck *you*. Can I interest you in a two-for-one offer?"

"Sixty-nine?" Taylan asked hopefully. "I heard that was the deal of the week."

Hudson wouldn't have thought retail chat could possibly have been used as dirty talk, but it was still turning his crank in a big way as he and Taylan laughed and scrambled around until they had the other's head between their legs.

"Satisfaction guaranteed," Hudson murmured as he slipped his lips over Taylan's glistening tip.

He wasn't sure what was better. The hot, salty taste of Taylan's hard, heavy cock sliding over his tongue, or how the way having his own cock in Taylan's mouth made his entire body shiver. He was tempted to thrust down, but he didn't know how Taylan sucked cock (yet), so he just allowed him to take charge of pleasuring him. Hudson was busy himself, after all, swallowing down Taylan's juicy length and massaging his heavy balls.

Hudson was tempted to come like this, but Taylan had asked – very nicely – to be fucked. So after a few blissful minutes, Hudson popped off Taylan's cock and kissed his inner thigh. "Turn over, gorgeous," he urged.

Taylan groaned and eased his mouth free of Hudson's throbbing dick. "Okay," he rasped, shifting so he was lying on his stomach, hugging a pillow under his head and chest.

Hudson had to pause and admire such a stunning sight. He moved to place a tender kiss on Taylan's cheek and brush his hair back from his forehead. "You're fucking beautiful, you know that?"

Taylan rewarded him with a pretty blush, peeking out from under those impossibly long eyelashes. "So are you."

Hudson preened. It wasn't often anyone called him beautiful. In fact, no one ever did. People – especially guys – thought he was too manly for that. But he really, *really* liked being beautiful for Taylan.

He caressed his lover's back and ass cheeks, giving the round flesh a playful squeeze. "Can I eat you out a little to help stretch you?" he asked. His cock was a bit on the large side, but he'd learned that he fucking loved rimming to warm his partners up. But not everyone liked it. Case in point, Taylan bit his lip and ducked his head.

"Oh, uh, you don't have to, if you don't want to," he mumbled.

Hudson chuckled and sucked on his finger, then slipped it between Taylan's cheeks. Taylan jerked and moaned as Hudson stroked his tight hole.

"I wouldn't have asked if I didn't want to," he said soothingly. "I love doing that. But only if you're into it?"

Taylan peeked coyly over his shoulder. "I tried it once. I think the other guy was maybe in a hurry, so it was just kind of weird. I'll try it again, though, if it's something you like?"

Hudson waggled his eyebrows at him, shimmying down the bed. "Oh, baby. You're gonna *love* it, I swear. Let me go to town on this gorgeous, perfect ass."

Taylan giggled and nodded. Hudson loved the fact he was trusting him. He pulled Taylan's cheeks apart with his hands, revealing his dark, musky hole. He was smooth and hairless, which made sense, considering Taylan cared for other people's hair all the time. Usually, Hudson didn't mind hairy intimate parts. That was just human, after all. But he had to say he enjoyed the slick glide of his tongue over Taylan's most intimate area.

He was going to take his time.

5

———

TAYLAN

Taylan was in heaven.

He'd lost track of time as to how long Hudson had been eating him out, but he was so turned on he didn't care. Hudson was relaxing his hole and stretching him out, and yet the rest of Taylan's body was taut and quivering with lust and anticipation.

He hadn't really felt much when he'd tried rimming before, but it probably made a difference that Hudson wasn't lying. From the way he was moaning and how long he was dedicating down there, it was clear he was having a great time licking and kissing and sucking Taylan's sensitive hole. Taylan humped his hard, leaking cock against the bedsheets and got totally lost in the sensation.

When Hudson pushed two fingers inside and stroked his prostate, Taylan almost combusted.

"Do you want me to fuck you like this?" he asked Taylan in a low rumble.

It was tempting. Taylan knew he could get the best angle on his knees. But this wasn't about one-off sex with a hookup. This was about connecting with Hudson.

He looked over his shoulder into Hudson's beautiful green eyes. "Could I ride you?" he asked breathlessly. He wasn't normally very bold during sex, but Hudson made him feel glorious. And why shouldn't he ask for what he wanted?

Hudson's eyes widened, and his mouth pulled into that stunning lopsided smile again.

"Hell yeah," he enthused.

He slid his fingers out of Taylan's ass and rolled onto his back, grabbing the condom box as he did. But Taylan reached out and stopped his arm with his hand as he sat up.

"May I?" he asked.

Hudson blinked and looked up at him for a second before arching up and claiming Taylan's mouth in a filthy kiss. Taylan could taste his own musk, and he was startled to realize he liked it.

"You're so fucking cute," Hudson growled, handing over the condom box. Then he stretched back down on the bed and laced his hands behind his head. "Do you want me to lie back and think of England?"

Taylan plucked a condom from the box, then tore open the wrapper. "How about you think of Turkey, sir?" he suggested instead, delighted when Hudson snorted with mirth. Taylan hadn't been one for role playing in the bedroom before, but he was having so much fun he wasn't sure why he hadn't tried it before.

Maybe, like with rimming, he'd had to wait for Hudson to come along and show him how to do it just right.

Rather than pull the condom out of its packet right away, Taylan decided to make certain that Hudson was good and hard for him by sneaking in another taste of his big, meaty cock. Taylan was slightly nervous about fitting it all inside him, but if he was on top, gravity would help.

So he took a few moments to suck and lick the top half while he stroked his hand over the bottom half, squeezing and twisting, making Hudson jerk and grunt. Taylan shivered as Hudson carded his fingers through his hair, guiding his head gently as Taylan worked.

He felt so loved and cared for, even though he was the one servicing Hudson in that moment. There was just something about the other man that put Taylan so at ease. He'd felt it at the barbershop, but now he knew for sure.

When Hudson was hard as steel and spit was dripping all over Taylan's hand, he came off the bobbing cock with a gasp, wiped the back of his dry hand over his mouth, then hastily rolled the condom down Hudson's length. Taking a second to smear lube over both Hudson's cock and his own ass, Taylan then straddled Hudson's hips and braced his hands on Hudson's broad chest. Hudson reached between them to angle his cock, and they gazed into each other's eyes as Taylan pushed his entrance against the tip.

They groaned and panted as Taylan gradually lowered himself down. Their skin was shimmering with perspiration, and little droplets splashed from Taylan's chest and hair onto Hudson's hard planes.

"Fuck, you feel so good," Hudson growled. He skirted his hands up Taylan's back, then leaned up to suck on one of Taylan's nipples, grazing his teeth over the hard nub.

Taylan dropped his head back in pleasure, the burn in his ass easing, leaving him with a delicious fullness. When he bottomed out, he dropped down and hugged Hudson to him for a moment as he caught his breath and adjusted to the intrusion. Hudson kissed his neck tenderly. He hadn't moved at all while Taylan had been pushing his way over his cock. Now he hummed and caressed up and down Taylan's ribs.

"You feel heavenly," he whispered, licking the shell of Taylan's ear. Taylan shivered and cried out, almost overwhelmed by sensation. "Let me know when you want to move. I'm going to fuck you senseless."

Taylan laughed weakly. "Not if I ride you senseless first," he said, rolling his body. Hudson scrunched up his eyes and hissed in pleasure, his big hands clamping around Taylan's hips.

"Both sound good to me," Hudson grunted, pitching his hips upward and hitting Taylan's prostate with the blunt head of his cock.

"Oh, fuck," Taylan spluttered. He dug his fingers into Hudson's chest and began to rock. "You feel amazing. Holy shit."

He wasn't going to last long, he could tell. He'd been sex- and touch-starved for too long, not to mention lusting after Hudson for months. He'd hardly dared get his hopes up that something might happen between them. But after so many late-night fantasies, the real thing was so much better, and Taylan was already coming undone.

"Touch my dick," he begged, needing release but not wanting to lose the support of leaning on Hudson's firm muscles. Besides, he wanted to feel Hudson everywhere, and his cock bounced happily as Hudson did as he was told and wrapped his fingers around Taylan's leaking length, jerking him roughly.

"You're fucking gorgeous, Taylan," Hudson said, digging his other fingers into Taylan's side. "I want you to come all over me with my dick in your perfect ass. I've wanted you for so long. Fuck, yes, harder!"

Taylan sped up as much as his burning thighs would let him, completely lost in Hudson's all-consuming touch and commanding voice. Hudson was rocking up to meet him, their damp flesh slapping and their breaths and grunts ragged as they chased their release.

Suddenly, Taylan's orgasm rushed over him, and he shuddered and cried out as he began shooting milky white cum all over Hudson's hand and chest. As he stilled, spilling his load, Hudson fucked him even faster, thrusting up into him with such force that Taylan bounced on top of him. Then Hudson arched up, burying his face against Taylan's neck, bellowing as he came.

His balls finally empty, Taylan stopped spurting, but his dick was still hard in Hudson's firm grip. He trembled as he struggled to keep himself braced against Hudson's chest, but then Hudson flung his arms around Taylan's back and hugged them together tightly, spreading the hot jizz between them. Gradually, Taylan felt Hudson's cock stop twitching and throbbing in his ass and eventually began to soften.

The only sounds were their panting breaths as they clung to one another in the dark. The soft glow of the streetlamps and Christmas lights shone through the slits in Taylan's blinds, but that was more than enough to see the deeply contented look on Hudson's face as they pulled apart and began to kiss luxuriously.

"Holy fuck," said Taylan after a minute.

Hudson chuckled. "My thoughts exactly. I guess I'll have to leave that five-star Yelp review after all, hmm?"

Taylan laughed, his heart rate slowing. He couldn't remember feeling this relaxed and sated ever. Hudson was like a balm for his body and his soul. "Five stars indeed," he agreed. Then he looked between them at all the goop. "I should go get us some tissues," he said with a weak laugh.

But Hudson shook his head and cupped the side of Taylan's jaw. "How about I take you into the shower? Then we can heat that pasta up in the microwave and snuggle on the couch."

Taylan's heart flipped like a trapeze artist. He'd been half-fearing that Hudson would just up and leave now he'd gotten off. "That sounds lovely," Taylan whispered, nuzzling his cheek against Hudson's palm. "Do you want to stay the night?"

Don't ask, don't get, right?

To his utter delight, Hudson's face broke into a warm smile, like sunshine piercing the clouds and lighting up fresh snow.

"I'd love that," he said.

Taylan bit his lip, then kissed Hudson softly. "So would I," he confessed.

There was a scratch at the door, and Taylan laughed, shaking his head. "So would a certain little madam, so it seems," he said with a sigh.

But Hudson didn't appear to mind at all. "Come on," he said. "Let's get ourselves decent, then we can fuss over Pom. She's been a very good girl." He caught Taylan's lip between his teeth for a nip. "And her daddy has been a *very* good boy."

Taylan blushed. "I…" he started, not quite sure what he was trying to say. Then he took a breath and looked Hudson in the eyes. "Next time you want to ask me for coffee, do it. I'll say yes. Anytime."

Hudson caressed the side of his neck. "Come with me to my family's New Year's party tomorrow. I think your friends will be there, too. It wouldn't be that big of a thing, like the club. It'll be cozy, and…well, I'd kind of like you to meet them outside of work."

Taylan's breath hitched. "You want to go together?" he asked, hoping he wasn't about to put his foot in his mouth. "You mean like…as a couple?"

But Hudson nodded, and Taylan's heart leaped. "As a couple," Hudson repeated. "If that's what you'd want?"

It was true that Taylan hadn't been able to face the idea of a club. But a family party, maybe as Hudson's date?

Hell yeah.

Taylan had begun that night feeling lonely and a little hopeless. Now he was in bed with his crush, being asked to be his boyfriend, officially.

He wasn't going to be alone on New Year's Eve after all.

"I'd love nothing more," he said sincerely.

EPILOGUE

Taylan – The Next Night

Taylan sort of knew that Hudson's dads, Sunny and Tyee Perkins, ran the diner on Main Street. Sunny Side Up was the heart and soul of Pine Cove, after all. But Taylan hadn't quite appreciated what a big family they had and how many close friends that also encompassed.

All three of Hudson's brothers, as well as his sister, were all either married or engaged, and had anywhere between one and three kids, some of whom were beyond hyper at being allowed to stay up until midnight. Taylan smiled and stepped out of the way as a pair of twin toddlers came racing past, squealing in delight.

Hudson slipped his hand over Taylan's hip and held him close. Immediately, Taylan relaxed. He didn't want to be stressed. He was having a wonderful time, really. But he wasn't used to this many people. "If you forget anyone's name, just step on my foot," Hudson murmured into his ear, making Taylan chuckle.

Apart from Hudson's siblings and their families, the Coal family was also there. That clan was almost as big as the Perkins lot, and between all their partners, kids, and best friends, it was no wonder Taylan was slightly nervous about forgetting some names.

The two families had been brought together because Swift Coal was BFFs with Rhett, one of Hudson's brothers. But Swift was also engaged to Micha, Hudson's baby brother, and the two looked so in love every time they were near each other. Before, that would have made Taylan feel a pang of sadness for what he was missing out on, but now…

…now he wondered if he might actually be falling in love. He'd certainly come to adore Hudson in the months he'd known him previously. But after last night, his heart was so impossibly full, Taylan felt it could only be the beginnings of love.

The room was bursting with it, and not just from the many couples that were there together, drinking and dancing at the Perkins' private affair. It was known in the town that Sunny and Tyee could make a killing if they opened up for a public party, but every year, they closed down the business to spend time with those who matter the most. Taylan had never even thought what it might be like to come to one of these get togethers. Taylan couldn't help but feel like a member of Pine Cove royalty as Hudson slowly introduced him to everyone. Not that a lot of people didn't know him already from coming into the barbershop.

But Hudson was making a point of introducing Taylan as his *boyfriend.* Taylan got a thrill down his spine every single time he heard that word and imagined it wouldn't wear off anytime soon.

Taylan loved how welcoming the crowd was. He was

surprised to learn that Swift's ex-girlfriend, Amy, was also in attendance with her boyfriend. She was the mother of Swift's daughter, and Taylan felt it was wonderfully modern how they all got along so well.

He'd been holding himself back from hanging out with Kamran and the others like Emery and the twins for so long, thinking he would be out of place. But that was the beauty of this gaggle of people. Everyone was a little different or out of place in their own way, and yet they were all so friendly and inclusive, no one was made to feel left out.

Taylan was so glad he'd stopped getting in his own way.

In his head, everyone here was coupled up, but that wasn't the case. There were a few other single people at the party aside from Kamran, including Jay Coal, although he seemed glued to his phone for most of the night and had FaceTimed with someone twice already.

When Hudson had asked Jay's twin, Robin, who he was talking to, Robin had rolled his eyes and said Hudson didn't want to know. Taylan wondered, though. When he thought no one was looking, there was a sadness in Jay's eyes that Taylan caught once or twice. Taylan felt like he knew that feeling all too well.

But not anymore.

Parting ways that morning so Taylan could go to his last day at work had been a kind of torture. But seeing as Hudson wasn't back to work until the following week, he'd gone home to pack a bag and had been there waiting for Taylan the moment his shift ended. They'd decided to spend a few days together to see how they felt, and already Taylan was the happiest he'd been in years. It just felt so *right* having Hudson in his life.

Pom certainly loved him.

That was the other good thing about closing the diner for a family-only function. Pom had been welcomed to join them, too, despite the usual health and safety regulations, and was having a blast scampering between Sunny and Tyee's old Great Pyrenees, Peri, as well as being chased around by all the younger kids. Emery Klein – a good friend of the twins, client of Taylan's, and a pretty famous social media influencer – had scooped Pom up for a photo shoot that he'd declared was already going viral.

The Champagne and other drinks were free flowing. Taylan felt bad not paying for anything, but Hudson insisted that was just the way these parties went. Besides food cooked by Sunny, Emery's friend, Ben Turner, had provided a whole table of delicious sticky goods from the bakery he owned here in town. Taylan had been introduced to his lawyer fiancé, Elias. They'd only gotten engaged just before Christmas, and Emery was excitedly bullying Ben into telling the elaborate story to anyone who would stand still long enough.

"I hope I'm that happy one day," Hudson murmured into Taylan's ear as he got them each fresh flutes of bubbly. "I'd like to think I'd plan a pretty decent proposal, too."

Taylan's stomach flipped. He knew he was being utterly ridiculous, but was it really so bad that he had a fleeting vision that maybe one day *he* would be the man Hudson got down on one knee for?

"What makes you think you'll be the one to propose?" Taylan asked playfully. He felt so relaxed with Hudson it was as if he forgot to worry or be anxious. He was still rusty when it came to people in general, but with Hudson by his side, guiding him, he felt like he was remembering how much he actually loved socializing.

Hudson hummed over the music and nipped at Taylan's earlobe. "You're right. I guess we'll just have to wait and see, won't we?"

Taylan's heart almost stopped beating. Of course Hudson

meant 'we' in a generic sense…but it was hard for Taylan not to imagine that he really *was* talking about them.

But why was it so bad to dream? Taylan had fantasized about Hudson for months, and now that was real. Maybe a proposal would be a reality someday down the line, too?

"Come on!" said Robin's excitable friend Peyton, raising her glass and pointing through the windows. "It's almost midnight! Let's head outside!"

Taylan caught Ava Coal, Robin and Jay's sister, looking forlornly at Peyton, but then the moment passed, and Ava stalked out the door, looking mildly menacing in her bike leathers, and Taylan wondered if he'd imagined the whole thing. Maybe once he got bolder, he would find out more of the group gossip from his friends.

He realized he'd actually really like that.

As he and Hudson shrugged their coats on and caught Pom to attach her leash, Kamran came and clapped Taylan on the shoulder. "I know I already said it, but we're really glad you came after all, buddy," he said warmly. He winked at Hudson and took a swig of his beer. "And with this big hunk on your arm, I'm impressed." He leaned in closer to the two of them. "Hey, if you guys ever want a third, just let me know."

Taylan blushed furiously as Kamran cackled. "Oh, uh," stammered Taylan.

"Thank you, however, we're good for now," Hudson said firmly but with a smile. "I'm enjoying this one all to myself and will be for a long time."

Kamran bit his lip and looked between them. "Ahh, I don't blame you. Anyway, the offer stands. Have fun, you crazy kids."

He punched Hudson's arm and pressed a surprisingly sweet kiss against Taylan's cheek. Then he scampered off, joining the crowd as they spilled out onto the main street to watch the fireworks over the lake, mingling with many others from the town.

"Can you see?" Jay asked his phone, turning the screen around so whoever was on the other end could look at the throng. "Second New Year's, coming right up!"

Whoever it was laughed and said something about time zones. Then Jay was gone.

Taylan looked at Hudson, who shrugged. Then he slipped his hand into Taylan's and led him out into the cold.

People were already counting down from ten, and Hudson joined in loudly as he wrapped his arms around Taylan, hugging him from behind and resting his chin on the top of Taylan's head. Pom sat obediently at Taylan's feet, and Taylan felt so deeply content and safe, despite being in a sea of people. The thought of this a couple of days ago would have freaked him out, but now he felt like Hudson was his anchor in a storm.

"THREE! TWO! ONE! HAPPY NEW YEAR!" the crowd bellowed as fireworks exploded in the midnight sky. But Taylan would watch them in a minute.

For now, he was kissing his new love, no longer alone, excited for the new year to come.

CALM SHORES

Gorgeous, sophisticated Dante walks into Oliver's bar and orders…a boyfriend?!

Dante needs a man to keep his mother from setting him back up with his awful, cheating ex. And Oliver wants a peek at the canapés and glitz of his life, so he jumps on the chance. Not on Dante, of course. That would be out of bounds…right?

Calm Shores is a stand-alone story featuring secondary characters from Pine Cove set after book #6: Thin Ice. 18K words.

OLIVER

"Wʜᴀᴛ ᴄᴀɴ I ɢᴇᴛ ʏᴏᴜ?" Oʟɪᴠᴇʀ ᴀsᴋᴇᴅ, sᴍɪʟɪɴɢ ᴘᴏʟɪᴛᴇʟʏ ᴀᴛ the tall drink of water that had just marched into Aquarium, looking somewhat flustered.

"A boyfriend?"

Oliver blinked. The man's thick, neat eyebrows crept up his face as he grimaced.

Apparently, Oliver had not misheard him.

He wiped down the bar in front of him out of habit, then flicked the dishtowel over his shoulder. "A boyfriend?" he repeated.

The guy shook his head, then looked around at the mostly empty bar. It was a Friday, but early enough that most people were still at work. Oliver was the only one manning the bar with a few patrons scattered around, including a couple of regulars he considered friends. Emery Klein was currently cackling at something Kamran Amir had just said over their collection of empty cocktail glasses on a nearby table.

No one else was close enough to Oliver and his newest customer, though, so he was left to puzzle alone over what the guy had just said.

"Yeah," said the guy uncomfortably. "A boyfriend." He sighed and loosened his tie. As a bartender in Pine Cove's one and only gay bar, Oliver was used to seeing many kinds of people there. But a three-piece suit was unusual, and he had to admit the newcomer had piqued his interest even before his strange request.

The guy slid onto one of the empty barstools and laced long, strong fingers together in front of him. Oliver considered himself a twink even though he was of a stockier build than some of his friends, but this guy was all man. Broad shoulders, well built, and a chiseled jaw with just the right amount of scruff. Oliver licked his lips and was glad that flirting was unofficially part of his job description.

"I'm not sure I can muster you up a boyfriend," he said with an impish smile, "but how about a drink?"

The guy blew out his cheeks. "I don't suppose you have a wine list, do you?"

Oliver dropped his head back and laughed. "Not an actual list, no. People tend to just ask for white wine spritzers. But why don't you tell me what you like, and I'll see what I can do?"

The guy considered him, and Oliver felt a little prickle over his skin. He didn't mind having this guy's attention on him, even if he was being judged as to whether or not he could recommend a decent glass of vino.

"Malbec," Mr. Suit said with a slight narrowing of his eyes.

Oliver preened. "We have a juicy malbec I bet you'll love," he said, spinning around and easily putting his hand on the bottle. "Hints of plum and mulberry, but not so much that the fruitiness overpowers the other flavors and makes it heavy." He sliced the foil off the top of the bottle and made short work of extracting the cork. He then poured a splash into a clean glass and gave it a little swirl. "Try that," he told Mr. Suit.

The guy's mouth quirked in what might have been amusement before he shrugged and picked up the glass with those sturdy fingers that made Oliver wet his lips again. The things he could imagine those fingers doing…

The guy blinked as he took a sip, then moved the glass in front of his face to marvel at the wine inside. "That's actually not half bad," he said.

Oliver scoffed. "Why, thank you," he said cheekily. "Not bad enough to warrant a full glass?"

The guy put the glass down on the bar and nodded. "God, yes. Make it a big one."

"Are you hoping to find a boyfriend at the bottom of it?" Oliver asked as he poured.

Usually, he didn't get to chat with customers as he was too busy racing from one to the next so that no one was waiting too long. He was glad that, for the moment, he was able to give Mr. Suit his full attention. Meeting new people was the best part of Oliver's job, after all. It had certainly done his sex life a lot of good.

Oh, fuck. If this guy would settle for a hookup rather than a boyfriend, Oliver would volunteer as tribute in a heartbeat.

Mr. Suit sighed again and looked around the bar. "I was hoping to find a date for this evening, yes," he said despondently. "It's usually packed when I come in here. But it's just my luck that in my hour of need the pickings are less than slim."

So he had been in Aquarium before? Oliver couldn't say he recognized him, but he must see hundreds of customers each week. Still, he'd like to think that he'd remember such a handsome face.

Oliver started slicing limes. It was easier to talk to such a hot guy when his hands were busy doing something else. Especially as he was about to up his flirting game.

"Surely a guy like you doesn't have trouble meeting men?" he said smoothly.

The guy scoffed and swirled his wine, watching the red liquid spiral. "Oh, I meet plenty of men," he said somewhat darkly. "It's finding ones that aren't total assholes that seems to be the tricky part."

Oliver laughed. "Tell me about it," he said, shaking his head. He'd dated some real charmers in his time, including the last one who had not only broken up with Oliver over text but also had stolen his fucking *TV* before he'd run off. It was why Oliver had been sticking to hookups recently.

Not that he didn't *want* a nice man to date. A grown-up with a real job and a car, the kind who did sensible things like pay taxes on time and romantic things like whisk Oliver out for fancy dinners and sexy things like fuck his brains out every night.

No wonder he was single. Men like that didn't exactly grow on trees.

"So what's so special about tonight?" he asked to keep the conversation going.

He still maintained that a guy like this could get a date in a flash, but apparently none of the guys in Aquarium were to his liking. Obviously, Emery and Kamran were both taken, but Mr. Suit didn't know that.

It made Oliver wonder what *was* Mr. Suit's type. Probably not Oliver, he thought with a pang, judging by his blingy watch that probably cost what Oliver paid his parents in rent for the whole year. Not to mention that Oliver's hair was dyed purple and teal, and his idea of a good time was eating nachos and watching anime. No, Mr. Suit was completely out of Oliver's league for anything other than a quickie in the men's room.

Which – to be clear – Oliver would absolutely not pass up.

"I have a big family dinner tonight at the Peaks Country Club," Mr. Suit said before taking a sip of his wine. The way he licked his lips after made Oliver want to moan, but he managed to keep control of himself. "My sister let it slip this morning that our mother has invited my douchebag ex behind my back because she wants us to get back together."

"Ouch," said Oliver sincerely, frowning as he scooped up his lime slices into the plastic tub for putting in drinks later. "And you don't want that?"

"To get back together with a two-timing sleaze bag?" Mr. Suit asked with an arched eyebrow that made Oliver's knees turn to water. It was so commanding and sexy. "I'd rather order a white wine spritzer from you."

Oliver snorted, appreciating the twinkle of mirth that danced in the guy's eyes at the playful joke. "If he's so awful, why were you with him in the first place?" he asked boldly.

Mr. Suit shook his head. "The sex was spectacular, but it was usually because I was pissed at him. Angry fucking can only get you so far, especially when he started fucking other people without telling me. But my mother *adored* him. He's a senior financial consultant for a big pensions firm in Seattle, and his family is old money. When I kicked him to the curb, she'd already picked out the wedding flowers." He grimaced and took another sip of wine. "Nothing seems to convince her that I fucking *hate* him."

"Wow," said Oliver. Without needing to be told, he picked up the wine bottle and topped up the guy's glass. His smile was sad, but there was also a hint of warm appreciation, or so Oliver thought. "And she's going to ambush you tonight? Does this douchebag even want to get back together with you?"

"Brian likes playing games," said Mr. Suit ruefully. "I'm

not sure he's capable of *loving* anyone, but he sure does like winning."

"But you don't want to play," Oliver guessed. "You figured if you innocently showed up with a 'new boyfriend' on your arm, your mom couldn't try and force you back together with the douchebag."

"Oh, she'll still *try*," Mr. Suit said, his dark eyes meeting Oliver's with an intensity that made Oliver's insides squirm. He felt like he was being allowed in on a secret with this handsome stranger, and he had to say he was reveling in it. "But I'd have an iron-clad excuse to shut her down and stay away from Brian."

Oliver smirked. "Worried about some of that angry sex, uh?"

Mr. Suit shook his head and looked irritably into his wine. "It's a distinct possibility," he growled, sounding frustrated with himself rather than Oliver for pointing it out.

"Who's having angry sex?"

Oliver had been so engrossed in his conversation he hadn't even noticed that Emery had approached the bar, carrying several different shaped glasses, all now empty of their various colorful concoctions. He placed them down, then looked between Oliver and his customer.

"Oh em gee, you're not angry with Oliver, are you?" he asked, scandalized. "He's the sweetest bunny rabbit!"

Mr. Suit laughed and gave Oliver a look that was most definitely warm. In fact, it bordered on smoldering. "No, Oliver – is it?" Oliver nodded. "Oliver was actually listening to my woes about my ex and reminding me that angry sex is never worth it. Not with Brian anyway."

"Sex with Oliver is *always* worth it, though," Kamran announced as he joined the conversation with a grin. He sighed and reached out to squeeze Oliver's arm good-naturedly. "I'm a one-man guy now, but Oliver and I sure had some fun before."

Oliver could feel himself start to blush fiercely. That was true, and he and Kamran were always friends first and hookups second, so he knew the compliment was genuine and friendly. But he knew Mr. Suit would *never* be interested in lowering himself to have sex with him.

Probably.

"That wasn't – this gentleman is looking for a *respectable* date for tonight so his mom would quit trying to get him back together with the awful ex so he doesn't have angry sex with *him*."

Emery looked between them again as Mr. Suit laughed gently at Oliver's summary of the situation. "And you came hunting in here?" he asked.

Mr. Suit shrugged. "I looked on a couple of apps, but it seemed kind of weird. Like I was auditioning someone to pretend to be my boyfriend. I thought if I could make a connection with someone, it would be slightly less weird to ask them on a date tonight. Then we could maybe stretch the truth a little as to how long we'd known each other." He looked morosely around as if hoping some new patrons had miraculously appeared in the time he'd been sitting down.

They hadn't.

"You mean a connection like you've made with our cutie Oliver here?" Emery asked, fluttering his eyelashes.

Oliver spluttered. "W-what? We were just, uh…"

"Flirting," Kamran supplied devilishly. "We noticed. You're lucky I managed to stop Emery from coming over before now, but I had to pee eventually."

Emery waved him off, his eyes sparkling as he grinned at Mr. Suit. "I just like to look after my friends," he said sweetly, and Oliver had to admit it was nice hearing Emery call him a friend. He spent so much time working his ass off behind the bar he wasn't sure if Emery or any of his other buddies really saw him like that.

Mr. Suit licked his lips and smiled, looking from his wine to Emery to Oliver. "Your friend has been very kind to me, but if I showed up to dinner tonight with someone with purple hair and tattoos, my mother might drop dead."

Ouch. Oliver couldn't help but scowl. He knew he wasn't in Mr. Suit's league, but that was kind of rude.

It seemed Emery and Kamran had a different take on Mr. Suit's comment, however. "Perfect," Emery declared. "You said you wanted your mom to stop with the douchebag matchmaking, yes?" He flicked his fingers elegantly, indicating Oliver like he was a gameshow prize. "Bring an adorable queer to charm the pants off your family, and either your mom will see that the evil ex is completely off the table, or it'll drive her crazy. Either way, you win."

Mr. Suit raised his eyebrows and tilted his head. "Actually…you might have a point."

He looked back at Oliver as if considering him in a new light, but anger rose in Oliver and he waved a finger at them both.

"Oh hell, no," he said firmly. "I am *not* some circus freak to be gaped at. My gender identity isn't a gimmick to be used against bigots."

Mr. Suit blinked as his jaw dropped open. "Of course not," he said, horrified. "I apologize."

But Emery scoffed. "Oh please, honey. Like you don't delight in baffling closed-minded folks every day? No one *here* would be making fun of you. Right?" Mr. Suit shook his head earnestly. "Think of it as…weaponizing your queerness for a good cause."

He grinned mischievously, and Oliver pursed his lips together to stop himself from smiling. When Emery phrased it like that, it kind of sounded fun.

But he shook his head. "I have to work," he said.

Trust Kamran to betray him. "Nuh-uh. You're only on until five, and then I was going to bully you into joining us for the rest of the night. I bet one of the other guys out back could cover for you if you wanted to leave right now."

Oliver opened and closed his mouth, glancing at Mr. Suit before scowling at his friends. "I'm sure the gentleman—"

"Dante," said Mr. Suit. Oliver blinked at him. Of course he had a sexy fucking name to go with that sexy goddamned body and face.

"Dante," Oliver repeated. "Dante is right. He doesn't want to go to a big fancy family dinner with some bartender he just met dressed in ripped jeans."

Dante sat up straighter in his seat, ignoring Emery and Kamran now, his eyes fixed on Oliver. "I completely understand if you wouldn't want to help me out. But if you did allow me to take you to dinner, you'd be doing me the hugest favor. Plus, I think we could have fun."

Was it Oliver's imagination, or did Dante look a bit bashful? Would he really *want* to take Oliver out?

He licked his lips. "I don't have any fancy clothes," he said honestly. Dante was clearly from money, and a family dinner was bound to be beyond anything Oliver was prepared for.

But Dante's eyes lit up. "It would be my *pleasure* to take you shopping, if you wanted?" He checked his expensive watch. "We still have time."

Emery's eyes lit up. *"Shopping?"* he hissed, nodding at Oliver. Clearly, he saw this as a bonus, but Oliver just wondered if it was Dante trying to make Oliver more palatable for his stuck-up family.

"It would be the least I could do if you would help me out," Dante said, his brown eyes full of damn sincerity.

"I…" Oliver said warily. "I don't know. That feels greedy or something. Like a payment?"

"So?" said Kamran.

"No, he's right," said Dante, shaking his head and looking crestfallen. "I've gone about this all wrong. I'm *so* sorry. That was exactly the kind of vibe I was trying to avoid. I'll just… this whole thing was a bad idea. I'm sorry." He pulled a twenty from his wallet – far too much for the glass of wine he hadn't even finished. "Thank you for listening to my woes," he said genuinely to Oliver. "I shall face the music alone. At thirty-five, I'm pretty sure I can muster up the courage to stand up to my mother."

Emery looked like he was going to protest, but Kamran elbowed him in the ribs. Oliver bit his lip as he watched Dante stand, and suddenly he wasn't in control of his own mouth anymore.

"Guys buy nice things for their new boyfriends all the time, right?" he blurted out. He swallowed as Dante met his eyes again and paused from walking away from the bar. "So, um, ask me out, Dante. Then I might accept a little present. And maybe I'll come meet your parents. Because I'm so…"

"Adorable!" Emery cried in delight.

"Smart," said Kamran with a salute.

Dante grinned, looking visibly relieved. "Oliver," he said, making his name sound so incredibly important. "May I have the pleasure of taking you to dinner?"

Oliver grinned back, not really believing he was doing this. "Of course, Dante. Let's go show your family how *madly* in love you are with your new boyfriend."

This was going to be fun.

2

———

DANTE

Was Dante insane?

In his fury at his mother and Brian, it had all seemed quite logical when he'd booked a car to take him to his hometown's one and only gay bar. He'd been there a few times over the years, although not so much recently. But when he'd walked through the doors that afternoon and only seen the seriously cute bartender, he'd started to suspect that he was acting like a crazy person.

But then he'd started talking with Oliver, with his teal-and-purple hair and his surprising knowledge of good wine, and Dante had started to believe he was wholly justified in bringing a spur-of-the-moment date to his cousin's big engagement party.

And now here he was, in the large department store in Penny Falls, insisting that he spoil his evening date for all the trouble he was putting himself to.

Dante felt like a complete asshole for implying that he'd *pay* Oliver for his services. That kind of thing was fine in other circumstances. Dante didn't judge – each to their own. But that wasn't what he'd wanted for tonight. He'd wanted a friend, and everyone he knew these days was back in Seattle. Anyway, Brian would never believe Dante was dating someone from his inner circle as he'd met them all. A stranger was the safest bet, and Oliver could really save Dante's neck by coming along and being his human shield.

He really wished he hadn't said that thing about Oliver's hair, though. It was a dick move that had clearly upset the young bartender. But Dante had to admit he was low-key obsessed with how someone could be that brave and bold to have their hair like that, and it really would cause a scene as far as his mother and other more conservative members of the family were concerned.

But Dante didn't want Oliver to think for one second that he was using him as some sort of gimmick. Dante had experienced enough trouble himself coming out in his twenties after he was done with college, fearing what his parents would do. His father had continued to pretty much ignore the fact until this day, but his mother had been quite excited. It made her somewhat edgy at the club with the other wives, and she'd enjoyed boasting about Brian the most to them.

Apparently, it didn't matter that he'd made Dante deeply unhappy. On paper, Brian was handsome, older, rich, and suave. The perfect conservative husband.

And completely the opposite of Oliver.

"Are you sure?" he asked as Dante placed a hand on his back and escorted him to the checkout with the bottle of aftershave they'd picked out. Dante had also treated Oliver to a double-cuffed shirt and cufflinks, but Oliver had assured Dante that he had a nice pair of pants at home as well as dress shoes. Dante didn't want to overwhelm him, but at the same time, he really wanted to show Oliver how grateful he was for the favor he was doing him.

The residual buzz from the wine was still running

through Dante's system, and he felt a little bold. So he leaned in and murmured against Oliver's ear, "Yes, you smell incredible."

As he pulled away, he saw Oliver bite his lip and blush. It looked amazing with his colorful hair, like Dante had his own human cockatoo for the night. A beautiful, rare exotic bird.

He tried to remind himself that they were just doing this for fun, that they didn't know each other, and this was mostly all pretend. But Dante couldn't deny the electricity he'd felt as soon as he'd laid eyes on the bartender only an hour or so ago. He had a smaller body type than Dante, but still solid. His tattoos on his arms were fun and had to have interesting stories behind them, and his eyes were such a dark blue they looked almost black.

He was extremely attractive.

But he was also doing Dante a huge favor, and therefore Dante was not going to make any kind of inappropriate moves on him or put him under any kind of pressure.

It was a beautiful summer's day as they stepped back outside of the shopping mall, and Dante marveled at how the colors in Oliver's hair shimmered. But Oliver caught him looking and self-consciously ran his hand through it.

"Sorry, it's not very subtle," he said with a wince.

Dante scowled, cursing his big mouth again. "It's gorgeous," he said firmly. He moved to stand them under the shade of a tree, its leaves rustling in the warm breeze. He looked Oliver directly in the eyes. "I apologize again for my insensitive words earlier. It's true that my mother won't approve, but her opinion doesn't matter to me, especially not right now. I think it's beautiful and a wonderful expression of who you are."

Oliver's eyebrows rose, and he stared at Dante for a second. "Um, thank you," he mumbled with a shy smile. "I know we've just met, but the point is to support you tonight. I guess I want to make sure my hair won't achieve the opposite of that. I can't believe your own mom would disregard your feelings so harshly."

Dante shrugged. Once he'd gotten over the initial shock of her audacity, it wasn't actually all that surprising that she would meddle like this. She was a woman used to getting her own way, no matter what.

"If you're worried about being a disappointment or something to my relatives, please don't." He smiled earnestly. "As far as I'm concerned, I've hit the jackpot with my emergency date."

He'd hoped Oliver might blush again, but instead, he frowned. "I'm a bartender who can't even afford to finish community college," he said quietly, averting his eyes.

Dante shook his head. "I've got a successful career in real estate that bores me to tears. I don't care about your job. Why don't I call a car, and we can talk more on the drive back to your place?" He touched Oliver's elbow and was rewarded with a small smile. "I want to hear what you do for fun. What your hopes and dreams are, your passions."

For a moment, Oliver just gaped at him.

"What?" Dante asked, worried he'd said something wrong again.

Oliver shook his head. "Sorry, I just…I guess I'm not used to people caring about that stuff. About, um, me."

Dante immediately wanted to ask why because Oliver was clearly a very interesting person. But he decided he didn't care. *He* wanted to know all those things about his new date, and if that meant he got Oliver to himself, that was just fine by him.

He used the private car service he had an account with to call a car. It was the same company he had a work account with, and he preferred it to a regular taxi or Uber. He figured he was still a bit of a snob despite disapproving of some of his family's ways. But Oliver didn't seem to mind the fancy car with its complimentary bottles of water and cool leather seats.

Dante was quickly coming to enjoy spoiling his date.

Oliver gave the driver his address. Then Dante began coaxing a few personal details out of him by asking about his tattoos. A number of them were inspired by anime TV shows that made Oliver beam as he talked about his love for them. He went dreamy-eyed as he mentioned how one day his dream was to visit Japan, and for a moment, Dante imagined them going together. Of course that was crazy – they'd literally just met. But no one had to know if he tucked the silly daydream away in his chest. He had a feeling that Oliver would be a fun person to go on vacation with.

"How about you?" Oliver asked, sounding genuinely interested rather than just being polite. "What do you do for fun?"

Dante smiled and glanced out the window at the neighborhood they were driving through. He'd grown up here as a kid with his cousins, but his family had moved for his father's work when Dante had been at middle school. It was nice to be back.

"I have some great friends in Seattle who I see a lot. We go to the theater and on bike rides on the weekends, things like that. When I need alone time, there's an indoor rock-climbing wall I go to regularly."

Oliver's eyes lit up. "I've always wanted to try rock-climbing."

Something warm unfurled in Dante's chest. "Maybe I could take you some time?" he asked. *On a real date,* he added to himself.

Would Oliver want to date for real? They lived in different places but…well, Dante decided to see how tonight went. If they had fun, perhaps they could talk about seeing each other again.

"Maybe," said Oliver with that shy smile that Dante was becoming very fond of. The things that did to his cock. He wanted to make Oliver blush and smile and bite his lip a whole lot more…

No expectations, he reminded himself. This was no ordinary first date, and he was going to keep his hands (and other body parts) to himself.

For now.

Oliver blinked and looked out the window. "Oh, we're nearly here. Do you, um, want to stay in the car? I'll be super fast. Five minutes tops."

Dante felt his eyebrows rise. "I mean, I can," he said. "But I don't mind if your place is a little messy, if that's what you're worried about?"

Oliver sighed as the driver came to a halt in front of a house on a street filled with decent-sized places and lots of pine trees along the sidewalk. "It's not that," he said. "It's… well, I live with my parents still. I'm saving for my own place." He winced and looked at Dante through his eyelashes.

But Dante shook his head and rubbed Oliver's arm. "I work in real estate, remember?" he told him kindly. "You don't have to tell me how difficult it is to get on the property ladder. Most young people stay with their folks or live with other people to try and get enough together to afford their own place. So please don't worry about that."

Oliver's shoulders dropped a little in relief. "Okay," he said sweetly.

"I'm okay to wait in the car if you'd rather I didn't come inside," Dante said truthfully. "But I'd also be happy to meet your family."

"Really?" Oliver asked dubiously.

Dante nodded. "You're throwing yourself into the lion's

den by meeting mine, and I can guarantee that yours won't be half as scary." He gave a half shrug. "It only seems fair."

For a moment, Oliver appeared to consider his options. Then he nodded with a lighter smile. "Sure, come on in," he said, opening his car door.

Dante asked the driver to please wait for them, then followed Oliver up the path through the front yard. He admired the neat, weed-free flower beds. Dante didn't know any of the flower names, but he smiled at the blue, red, and purple petal heads that bobbed at him like they were saying hello.

"My dad's crazy about gardening," Oliver explained as he juggled his shopping bags to get his key out. "He runs the hardware store in town, and he's always outside tinkering with stuff."

Dante wasn't sure his father had gotten his hands dirty a day in his life. He respected practical people.

"It's lovely," he told Oliver. They shared a smile that made Dante's heart flip in his chest, but then Oliver was opening the door to the house.

"I'm home!" Oliver called as he stepped through the front door into a cluttered entrance hall.

Shoes and boots were piled up on a rack, several umbrellas were jammed into an old metal stand, and dozens of coats and jackets vied for space on a number of hooks. Photos of Oliver covered the walls, as well as an assortment of academic achievements from Pine Cove High. There were certificates from spelling bees and debate competitions as well as outstanding contributions in music and drama.

Dante had been right. Oliver was definitely an interesting person. Dante wished he could take his time to study everything on the walls, but at that moment a tall, willowy woman emerged from what looked to be a kitchen, wrapping a chunky knit cardigan around herself despite the heat of the day outside.

"I thought you were working tonight, sweetheart," she began. Then she stopped, her eyes growing wide at the sight of Dante standing in her entranceway. "Oh, hello? Ollie, I didn't know you were bringing company over."

Aw, his mom called him Ollie? Dante liked that.

Oliver shook his head and went over to hug the woman whom Dante assumed to be his mother.

"I'm sorry, Mom. It's all very sudden. Dante has asked me out tonight, and we dropped in so I could freshen up. We'll be out of your hair in no time." He let her go and stood between them. "Mom, this is Dante. Dante, this is my mom, Katie."

Oliver's mom beamed at Dante, her eyes sparkling. "A date? Oh, how nice. Yes, you go ahead. I'll look after your young man." She bustled over to Dante, and to his complete shock, threw her arms around his neck and patted his back as she hugged him.

He'd met some of his friends' folks before, but none of them had ever been so friendly so fast. Considering his own mother was more icicle than human, he was just a little thrown.

"Mom," said Oliver in exasperation.

"Sorry," she said with a laugh as she released Dante. "It's just been a while since Ollie brought home a young man. And you're way more handsome than the last one!"

"*Mom,*" Oliver cried, covering his eyes with the hand not holding all the shopping bags. "Okay, I'm going for a thirty-second shower. The faster I am, the sooner we can leave."

Dante chuckled as he watched Oliver race up the stairs. Then he glanced at Katie and offered her a polite smile. "I can just wait in the living room out of your way," he said, indicating the doorway opposite him where he could see a sofa and coffee table.

But Oliver's mom frowned and shook her head. "Don't be silly. I'm delighted to have a friend of Ollie's over. Can I get you some coffee? The pot's fresh."

It was Dante's instinct to decline and hide himself out of the way, but that felt rude. Besides, Katie appeared genuine in her happiness for her son, so he didn't feel too awkward accepting. "That would be great."

She beamed and led him into a rustic-looking kitchen with wooden finishes and lots of red appliances. The fridge was covered in magnets, photos, letters, flyers, takeout menus, movie ticket stubs, and other various paper items stretching back several years, from the looks of it. Colorful teapots sat on the windowsill, and a ceiling fan spun lazily overhead.

Before Dante could blink, there was a steaming mug of black coffee being placed in front of him at the wooden table, along with cream and sugar in a chipped, matching set of pots and a slice of carrot cake on a small plate.

Dante stared at it. "That's my favorite," he said without thinking.

Katie practically danced on her toes before she dropped into the seat opposite him with her own coffee and cake. "I love that British baking show," she gushed, watching Dante fix his coffee with a dash of cream and a spoonful of sugar. "I'm always trying to perfect the recipes I see on there. Mine never look as pretty as theirs, but I think I've cracked this mix finally."

Dante didn't mean to, but an embarrassing moan vibrated in his throat as he took a bite of perfectly moist, slightly spicy cake. The frosting was rich and creamy, balanced by the juicy morsels of dried fruit.

"Wow," he said, covering his mouth as he finished

chewing and swallowed. "That's one of the best carrot cakes I've ever tasted."

Katie's eyes shone with tears, and for a second, Dante was horrified, not knowing what to do. He wasn't used to an overabundance of emotion. That was considered weakness in his family. But then Katie grinned and blinked until the wetness was gone.

"You've just made my day," she said happily. "Thank you. Now, what are you boys up to tonight? Oh no – are you going for dinner? I don't want to spoil your appetite!"

Dante laughed and pulled his plate closer to him protectively. "Nope, you can't have it back," he said playfully. "I'll just skip the appetizer later."

Katie sighed, wrapping her hands around her coffee mug. "You seem lovely," she said, completely unguarded. "I hope you and Ollie have a nice time. He deserves something special. It's been a while, and his last boyfriend was just awful."

"So was mine," Dante grunted, spearing his cake a little too forcefully.

For a second, he had a wild idea to blow off the dinner and just take Oliver somewhere fancy where they could be alone. A real date. But he actually liked his cousin Rebecca and wanted to celebrate her engagement with her, even if that meant putting up with seeing Brian's smug, arrogant face again.

He bit his lip, fighting the urge to tell Katie the truth. But she didn't need to know that this date tonight was sort of a fake. If Dante was lucky, he could see Oliver again soon under genuine circumstances.

If he was unlucky, dealing with Dante's family would be too much for Oliver, and he'd run for the hills. The thought made Dante's insides twist. But that was crazy. He'd only known him a couple of hours. If they parted ways after the event tonight, it would be no big deal, right?

But as Dante sat chatting with Oliver's sweet mom, eating her homemade cake, and listening to funny little stories about her son, Dante had the sneaking suspicion that it would be a very big deal indeed if he never saw his beautiful exotic bird again.

3

OLIVER

THE PEAKS COUNTRY CLUB WAS THE PLACE MOST PEOPLE HAD their big fancy events in Pine Cove. Weddings, anniversaries, milestone birthdays, school proms – basically anytime folks wanted to get dressed up and let their hair down, this was where you booked. Having been here several times before, Oliver would have thought it would start losing some of its charm by now, but as he and Dante approached in the private car, he realized it was still just as beautiful as ever.

The evening sunshine was strong, but fairy lights covered the entire log cabin-type structure as well as the surrounding trees, ready to glow as soon as twilight came in. Lush flowers in every color of the rainbow blossomed from meticulously kept beds and hanging baskets, and white classical sculptures of beautiful women peeked out from the shrubbery.

Most impressive, though, was the jewel of the town – the lake. It stretched out beyond the dock attached to the club, surrounded in the distance by pine forests and looming mountain tops. Rowboats bobbed on the calm shore, and Oliver imagined what it would be like for him and Dante to take a trip out over the water.

Then he bit his lip and reminded himself that this wasn't really a date. It was more like a mission, as Emery had said. He was weaponizing his queerness to protect Dante from his interfering mother and awful ex-boyfriend.

Dante had been really nice to him, though. He suspected the mini shopping spree was his way of trying to make up for putting his foot in his mouth about Oliver's hair. Not that Oliver had a shirt as fancy as this in his own closet. The fit and feel of it were amazing, and he loved how the opal cufflinks caught the sunlight. He felt a bit like Julia Roberts in Pretty Woman, but in a *good* way.

Dante had seemed sincere outside the mall when he'd said he really did like Oliver's hair. It was possible that he could mean that *and* like the idea of it pissing off his controlling mom. But they still didn't really know each other, and this wasn't really a date. It was more like a favor and Dante had bought Oliver a couple of gifts for his trouble.

In real life, Dante was still completely out of Oliver's league.

Except Oliver could have sworn he felt a little chemistry between them, different from the lustful spark at the bar. It was one thing to be attracted to someone and want to jump their bones for a quick release. But when Oliver had come downstairs to find Dante and his mom looking so cozy, drinking coffee and laughing, he couldn't help but wish with a physical pang in his heart that he and Dante were really a couple on a date.

And that had been before Dante had turned around to look at Oliver and his jaw had dropped. For a second, he hadn't said anything at all, leaving Oliver feeling self-conscious that his outfit wasn't good enough despite the fancy new shirt and expensive cologne. But then Dante had risen to his feet and touched Oliver's shoulder, telling him he looked gorgeous.

Of course, he could just be playing the part of doting boyfriend in front of Oliver's mom. It had been so long since anyone had paid any attention to Oliver that he was probably seeing things that weren't there and grabbing hold of any compliments that came his way. Dante needed a human shield for the evening, and because Oliver had agreed to be a good sport, Dante was simply being nice to him because of it.

Right?

There were a lot of people milling around in the entrance lobby. The main room was through an arch made out of roses where a couple seemed to be greeting guests as they went in to be seated for the dinner. From the looks of people's ages, there was a mix of family members and friends. Oliver recognized a few faces from his time at school, although he wasn't well enough acquainted with anyone to know their names or say they were actually friends.

"So your family is from here?" he asked Dante as they accepted glasses of red wine from a passing server.

Dante nodded and took a sip of his own glass. Oliver tried not to obsess over his glistening lips and how kissable they looked.

"I moved away when I was thirteen," Dante said. "But my aunt and uncle stayed with their kids, so we came back and visited a lot. In some ways, this feels more like home than Seattle."

Oliver felt a silly sense of pride at that. He loved his hometown, he had to admit. It meant something to him that Dante still liked it, too.

"Oh, shut the front door. You really did it!" a voice hissed, making Oliver turn around. A voluptuous woman with a cascade of red curls and a slinky dress approached them, looking delighted. "You got a date?"

Dante beamed at the woman. "I did. You're a lifesaver for the heads-up. Jilly, this is my 'boyfriend,' Oliver. Oliver, this is my hero of a sister, Jilly, who discovered our mother's wicked scheme in the nick of time."

"You look like Jessica Rabbit," Oliver said before he could stop his stupid mouth. He wasn't attracted to women at all, but he'd be blind not to see how gorgeous Dante's sister was.

And Oliver had just compared her to an eighties cartoon. Real classy and mature.

Expect Jilly laughed and touched her chest, seeming charmed. "What a compliment, thank you! You heard that, Dante? Your new boyfriend has taste!"

"He's buttering *me* up, not you," Dante said playfully. Then he hugged Oliver to his side, and Oliver's heart skipped a beat. *It's just for show,* he tried telling himself. But was the way Dante rubbed his thumb against Oliver's hip *really* for show? Jilly knew they were sort of faking it, and no one else was close enough to notice.

Was Dante actually flirting with him?

"Dante! There you are. I was starting to worry. I…"

The woman's voice trailed off as Dante turned with his arm still around Oliver. Jilly moved to his other side, making Oliver feel like he had a protection detail.

The woman was shorter than them all, dressed in a pale pink fitted dress with a matching cropped jacket and a set of very real-looking pearls around her slender neck. Her ash-blonde hair was styled in a bob just above her shoulders, and her nails were manicured professionally. Her expression faltered ever so slightly as she took in Dante's arm around Oliver's back, but then she was smiling brightly again as if nothing was amiss.

It was difficult to miss the hulk of a man beside her. She had her hand placed on his large arm, which he'd somehow stuffed into a black tux. Where Dante was big in a way that made Oliver crave his strong, masculine arms around him, this guy was big in a scary 'please don't hurt me' kind of way. His expression was caught somewhere between a scowl and a smirk as his eyes darted between Dante and Oliver. It made Oliver want to shrink away, but just at the right moment, Dante squeezed him to his side, and Oliver didn't feel quite so intimidated.

This had to be Brian. It wasn't in the least bit helpful, but Oliver's first thought was that angry sex between him and Dante must have been like a gladiatorial battle. Nothing like the kind of sex Oliver could ever offer. If that was what Dante was into, Oliver didn't stand a chance.

Except...he *wasn't* into that, was he? It hadn't been enough to keep them together as a couple, and Dante had come to Oliver's work specifically looking for someone to act as his boyfriend tonight to make sure he didn't slip back into bad habits and do something stupid.

This guy was the enemy, and it was Oliver's job to protect Dante from him.

"Mother," Dante said warmly, confirming Oliver's suspicions about the woman's identity. "You look stunning, as always." He then flicked his gaze to the mountain man and narrowed his eyes. "Brian. I didn't realize you were going to be here."

"Oh, of course," said Dante's mother with a laugh, rubbing Brian's arm. Oliver couldn't be certain, but he wondered if she was enjoying groping his muscles a little too much. "Brian is practically family."

Jilly stuck her lower lip out and frowned at her mom. "I thought it was kind of the *opposite* when your partner discovers you're screwing around and breaks up with you. Isn't that when you're specifically *no longer* part of the family?"

She batted her eyelashes and smiled sweetly at her mom, who looked thunderous for a second before laughing it off.

"Oh, nobody cares about that silliness," she said brightly. "Brian was so looking forward to catching up with you tonight, Dante."

She fixed Oliver with a pointed glare, like he should just melt away and leave Dante to his mom's scheming.

Oliver clung to Dante's arm tighter.

"I'm not sure we have much to catch up on," said Dante pleasantly. Then he beamed down at Oliver with such warmth he melted a little anyway for entirely different reasons. "Mother, I'd like you to meet Oliver. We've been seeing each other for a while now, and I'm delighted to introduce him to the family this evening. Oliver, this is my mother, Francine. And this is Brian."

Oliver kind of loved that Dante didn't even acknowledge Brian as his ex, so Oliver ignored him as well in favor of holding out his hand for Francine to shake. "It's a pleasure to meet you—" He faltered. He didn't know Dante's last name – *shit!* He swallowed the 'Mrs.' he'd almost just said. "Francine," he managed to utter instead. "Congratulations to your niece, Rebecca, and her husband-to-be."

He had no idea if that was the right thing to say, but it was the politest thing he could muster.

Francine's gaze was apparently stuck on Oliver's hair, but then she seemed to shake herself and held out her hand to Oliver to take. He suspected it was done through sheer politeness, however, as her eyes were cold and her smile tight, and he pumped her hand once, then released her again.

"Darling, you really should have checked first," she chastised as she looked back at her son. "This is Rebecca's special day. She should have been able to approve all the guests."

Jilly scoffed and snagged a glass of Champagne from a

passing tray. "This is Rebecca *and* Louis's event, and the special day will be their *wedding.* This is just an excuse for Uncle Alan to throw a big party, and *he* certainly won't care who Dante's date is so long as everyone's having a good time." She grinned and downed half her glass in one big gulp.

Francine adjusted her jacket and sniffed. "There's no need to be vulgar, Jillian. It won't impress anyone."

"I think she's hilarious," said Dante cheerfully. "Oh look, they're calling us in to be seated." He nodded at the block of granite known as Brian. He was still scowling, so Oliver wasn't sure if his feelings had changed since finding out Dante was there tonight with a date, but he certainly didn't look happy. "Maybe catch you later," he said with a tone that suggested that was the last thing he wanted.

But Oliver didn't care. Because then Dante swept him away from Brian and Francine toward the main room with a buoyant Jilly by their side.

"You did it," she whispered, squeezing both their shoulders as they joined the small line to greet the happy couple. "Now you can just enjoy the rest of the night."

"I didn't do anything," Oliver protested in a small voice. "I just stood there."

But Dante squeezed him tightly. "And looked gorgeous by my side while my mother was her usual rude self. *Thank* you. I mean it when I say you've already done me such a huge favor." They shared a look that made Oliver's heart tumble over in his chest with warmth and hope and longing.

Oliver wasn't sure it was going to be that easy for them to dissuade Francine. But for now, they had made it through the first encounter and come out on top, so Oliver was going to call that a win.

He wouldn't feel like they'd come out truly victorious until they left the party at the end of the night. But for that moment he had a nice glass of wine and was on the arm of a gorgeous man.

Things could be worse.

Much worse.

4

DANTE

Of course it wasn't that simple. Guests were seated, and somehow Dante's mom had finagled it so that Brian was on the same table as him. But Dante wasn't operating alone, and Jilly had worked her magic with Rebecca to ensure that he had a space for a plus-one seated beside him. Brian was still across the table, but at least Dante could keep Oliver close to him this way.

Plus, the wine was free flowing, which helped immensely.

The appetizer was civilized enough. Jilly was on Dante's other side, proudly single and happy to keep the conversation going with the several people around them. They had a mix of the happy couple's friends as well as an aunt and uncle from the groom's family. For a while, they all chatted happily about how they knew Rebecca and Louis, sharing funny anecdotes.

"How do you like the soup?" Dante murmured to Oliver. He was sipping each spoonful so carefully like he was terrified of splashing a drop on his new shirt or the white linen on the table.

Oliver licked his lips and gave Dante his now-familiar shy

smile. "It's delicious," he said earnestly. "I kind of thought tomato soup was just something out of a can, but this is amazing."

Someone laughed. Unkindly. Dante's hackles rose before he looked over to Brian, who was gracefully wiping the corners of his mouth with a napkin. "So I guess a lot's changed in a year," he said in a deep booming voice that automatically caught the attention of everyone else at the table.

"I guess it has," said Dante simply, not wanting to encourage him. He slipped his arm around Oliver's back possessively. Yes, technically, Oliver was the one acting as the buffer here. But Dante wasn't going to stand by and let Brian insult him like he was inevitably going to.

Sure enough, Brian arched an eyebrow and smirked. God, how had Dante ever found him attractive? Sure, objectively speaking, he was handsome and aging well as he went into his forties, but there was absolutely no kindness behind those eyes.

"How did you two meet?" Brian asked, fixing Oliver with his stare. The serving staff were clearing the table, but Brian ignored the waitress by his side completely, meaning she had to awkwardly reach around him to take his soup bowl.

Oliver, on the other hand, smiled at his waitress as she removed his crockery. "Thank you," he said to her first, then looked back at Brian. Dante felt him lean against his hand, so he rubbed little circles with his fingers, assuring Oliver that he was right there for him. "We met at the bar where I work. Dante came in one day, and we swapped numbers."

Brian blinked and looked between Oliver and Dante. "Oh…you work in a *bar?*" he said, the amusement clear in his voice.

"Bar work is super hard," Jilly piped up cheerfully, but Dante didn't miss her challenging tone. "I did it for a whole summer to afford a Hermès clutch Daddy wouldn't buy me." She preened and showed them all a hand-sized coral-pink bag. "And I *so* did it."

Brian held his hands up. "Oh, yeah, totally. I'm just surprised." He grinned and nodded his whiskey tumbler toward Dante. "That's just quite a change in circumstances for you."

Dante felt his temper flare, but Oliver sat up a little straighter beside him. "From what I've heard, Dante was in desperate need of a change," he said sweetly.

Jilly snorted. Some of the other guests looked a little uncomfortable, but Dante's heart swelled with pride. He was sure it had taken Oliver a lot of guts to stand up to Brian even that much after the way he'd talked about his insecurities.

But the truth was that Dante would rather be there that evening as Oliver the Bartender's date than Brian the Senior Financial Consultant's a thousand times over. He didn't care that Brian's credentials far outweighed Oliver's on paper. Oliver was kind and brave and sexy as hell.

Brian could go jump into the lake for all Dante cared.

The conversation was interrupted by the serving of their main course, and Jilly seized the opportunity to ask some of their cousin's friends what they did for a living. Dante joined in for a while, then turned his attention back to Oliver to ask him what made him want to try rock-climbing. It turned out that he'd done it a couple of times before as a teen after he'd seen it at the Olympics – both indoor and out – but he'd been thinking for a while about trying a course to get better.

Dante couldn't help but feel hopeful. It had to mean *something* that they already had a potential hobby in common. He delighted in telling Oliver about some of the walls he usually went to and explaining why certain ones were harder than others.

Oliver's eyes sparkled as they talked quietly, the rest of the party slipping away as far as Dante was concerned. It might as well have been just the two of them, exactly how Dante had wished for their first date.

After he had eaten all he wanted of his main course, Dante's hand naturally gravitated back to Oliver's warm, firm body, this time resting easily on his thigh. They drank their wine as the conversation moved to what Oliver had been studying at the community college in Penny Falls. He didn't actually have that many credits left to get before he could graduate, from the sounds of it, but when his mom had gone through a period of illness a couple of years ago, he'd put it all on hold to help take care of her.

Like Dante had already suspected – he was a sweetheart.

"I don't even know what I'd want to do once I get a degree in English Lit," Oliver said, shaking his head and drinking a little more wine. Dante liked the way it made his throat bob, and he shifted slightly in his seat where his cock was definitely interested in what Oliver and his mouth could maybe do later. "But I started it, so I want to finish it, you know?"

Dante nodded. "Absolutely," he agreed. Once he committed to something, he saw it through, no matter what. He appreciated that Oliver had the same mentality.

"I know it costs money," Oliver continued, "but I figure once I graduate, it'll help my job prospects. I like tending bar, but not forever. I want a regular daytime job so I can see my friends in the evening. And, um, maybe a boyfriend."

"Sounds good," Dante said, stroking Oliver's thigh with his thumb. In his mind, he'd already cast the role of the boyfriend, naturally.

"Do you think you'll stay in real estate?"

The question caught Dante off guard, although it wasn't that strange, considering they were discussing Oliver's career. It was more that Dante had admitted out loud to him earlier that what he was currently doing bored him to tears, which was something he rarely allowed himself to acknowledge.

"I'm not sure," he said, considering his wine as he organized his thoughts. "The company I work for in Seattle is huge. I've been wondering for a while if I wouldn't be suited to something more intimate, with more personal interaction with clients."

"Like in a small town?" Oliver asked.

Dante blinked, then glanced out the huge windows at the evening settling over the lake and the rest of Pine Cove. "Maybe," he said sincerely. He loved his friends, but the city wasn't that far away. Could a relocation to somewhere like his hometown be what he was looking for?

Or not 'somewhere like.' Would he consider moving back to Pine Cove? His cousins were here, after all.

Oliver was here.

He scoffed and realized how much wine he'd probably had by now. But it was so smooth, and Oliver was fun, easy company. Dante had even forgotten all about Brian as they'd eaten their entrees and desserts, and now the staff were bringing around Champagne, presumably for a toast.

Dante reminded himself that he'd promised to be a gentleman and not push too hard with Oliver, despite what his cock was urging him. So he reached for the glass pitcher of water and poured himself a tumbler to gulp down.

"I need to use the bathroom," he said quietly to Oliver. "Will you be all right by yourself?"

Oliver smiled, but the shyness had been replaced by something much flirtier. "I think I can manage a few minutes out of your sight," he said, batting his eyelashes. "Somehow, I'll survive."

Dante didn't think. He just tickled his ribs. "Cheeky," he

growled as Oliver laughed and squirmed. Then Dante leaned in closer, resting his hand on the curve of Oliver's hip. "I'll hurry back," he murmured and was rewarded by feeling Oliver shiver.

Smoothing down his shirt, vest, and jacket, Dante made his way to the men's room at the back of the room. The servers had almost finished distributing the glasses of Champagne to all the guests, and he didn't want to miss the speech from his cousin and her new fiancé. So he hurried to relieve himself and wash his hands, drying them on one of the small towels from the basket under the mirror, then dropping it into the wicker basket.

Just as he reached for the door, it swung inwards.

And Brian walked in.

Dante came to a stop in surprise as Brian used his bulk to block the door. *"For fuck's sake,"* Dante muttered. In the brief moment the door had been opened, he'd heard enough to realize Uncle Alan was introducing Rebecca, and here Brian was, trying to start something.

"Baby," Brian admonished, opening up his arms. "Come on. What's gotten into you tonight?"

"Nothing other than the desire to get back to my date and raise a toast to my cousin's wedded bliss. If you'll excuse me…" He tried moving to the left, but Brian moved as well. Dante scowled. "It's *over*, Brian. Fuck – it was toxic while it lasted anyway. You don't really want to get back together."

"Oh, but I do want *something* from you," Brian said, his voice dropping even lower as his gaze skated over Dante's body, lingering on his crotch.

A wave of nausea rolled over Dante. "Not if you were the last man on Earth," he snarled, pushing past Brian to get to the door. "You repulse me."

"Like that little freak could ever measure up to me?" Brian snapped, making Dante pause in the doorway. "You can't have fucked him yet. You'll come to your senses once you do. It'll be like fucking a *woman*, I'm sure." He stepped closer. "You need a *man* to take care of you, baby."

He rested his hand on Dante's shoulder, but Dante shrugged him off furiously before spinning around and pushing him back into the bathroom. He didn't want their voices traveling while Uncle Alan was talking into the microphone in front of the whole crowd.

"Don't fucking touch me again," Dante growled, shoving his finger in Brian's face. "And keep your gross, misogynistic opinions to yourself. Oliver is twice the man you are. Fuck you, you cheating, manipulative asshole."

"Jesus Christ," said Brian with a laugh, holding up his hands. "What the hell is this? Your time of the month? Okay, maybe I *don't* wanna fuck you, you pussy."

"However will I go on?" Dante said dryly before turning on his heels and marching out of the bathroom.

He'd intended on making a beeline back to Oliver on their table, but he saw his mother through the doors out to the lobby, and his already hot temper flared. As much as he wanted to support his cousin, he could speak to her in person later. Right now, he had the chance to be alone with his mother, and he needed to get something off his chest.

Ignoring everyone and everything else, he strode across the back of the room out into the lobby, following where his mother was walking out the front door, typing furiously on her phone despite her long, pointy gelled nails.

"Mother," Dante said briskly.

She paused and blinked at him before beaming. "Dante. What are you doing—"

He waved his hand to cut her off. "I don't appreciate you dragging Brian back into my life and respectfully ask that you never do it again."

She looked so wounded he almost felt sorry for her.

Almost.

"But he *adores* you," she protested. "Can't you forgive him? Everyone makes mistakes. Nobody's perfect, not even you."

"I don't need perfect. I need someone who loves me," Dante told her. "Someone who respects me."

She laughed. "And I suppose that colorful young man you brought tonight fits the bill? Honestly, darling, I was so embarrassed. What am I supposed to tell people? That you lost a bet?"

Dante gritted his teeth, then smiled. "I couldn't care less what you tell anyone. Oliver is my boyfriend, and I cherish him. If you want to keep me around, you're going to have to accept him, too."

He was probably being ridiculous. Who knew what future lay ahead for him and Oliver? They certainly weren't boyfriends.

Not yet.

But it felt really, *really* good to genuinely tell his mother that if she didn't accept Dante's boyfriend, she didn't get to have Dante either.

"Now, stop being silly," she said, but her expression told Dante that she wasn't convinced he was bluffing.

Good.

"Enjoy the rest of your evening, Mother," he said with a nod. Then despite her spluttering protests, he turned on his heel and finally made his way back to his table.

Except when he reentered the room and his eyes immediately searched for Oliver's striking teal-and-purple hair, his chair was empty, and he was nowhere to be seen.

5

OLIVER

This was too good to be true, surely?

Despite the blip with Brian's rudeness, Oliver was having such an amazing evening. Dante was giving him his undivided attention, and the feel of his hand resting on Oliver's leg was the stuff of dreams. He was funny and charming and made Oliver feel as if he was the only guy in the world.

Had they accidentally ended up on a real date? Possibly.

The room had a sense of anticipation about it as the newly engaged couple prepared to give a speech. Oliver hoped Dante would be back in time.

He'd had a few glasses of wine and was feeling pleasantly buzzed. So maybe that was how he missed Brian dropping into Dante's empty seat beside him. Oliver froze, his eyes instinctively darting to find Jilly, but she was speaking to her cousin, the bride-to-be.

Oliver was all alone.

"You can give up now," Brian said with a nasty grin, leaning in just a bit too closely. His breath smelled of strong whiskey and cigars, and Oliver flinched away.

"Give up what?" he said defiantly.

Brian chuckled. "The idea that you're any competition for me."

Oliver swallowed and rubbed his thumb against the wine glass stem. "It's not a competition. Dante doesn't want to be with you. He said you cheated on him and treated him badly."

Brian laughed darkly again and ran a finger along Oliver's arm. He snatched it away. *Gross.*

"What can I say?" Brian purred. "I'm a bad guy. But Dante loves it. So you stay here while I go remind him of that fact." He flicked his eyes up and down Oliver. "You might want to see if you have a friend who can come pick you up. You know, if you can't afford a cab."

Red hot humiliation rushed through Oliver's entire body, rendering him mute. He trembled as he watched Brian stand and button his jacket before casually strolling across the room toward the bathroom.

Oliver licked his lips, feeling dizzy, and looked around the table. But it seemed that his and Brian's conversation had been quiet enough that none of the other guests had noticed. He took a few deep breaths and gripped the edges of his seat, trying to center himself.

Brian was full of shit. Dante had made it clear that he hated him and wanted nothing to do with him.

He'd also admitted that the angry make-up sex had been so hot it had basically kept them together way longer than they should have been. It was supposed to be Oliver's job to act as a buffer between them, to keep Dante safe. Yet he'd let Brian follow him into the men's room.

Oliver didn't care that Brian was older and much bigger than him. He'd made a promise and cared about Dante, even after just a few hours. He needed to stick to his mission and do his job.

Carefully, he folded up his napkin and placed it on the

table in front of him, then took a big gulp of red wine to fortify his courage. He was just going to go tell Dante that the speeches were starting because they really were about to. A man who was probably somebody's father was tapping a spoon on a glass, the gentle ringing getting everyone's attention. Oliver used the opportunity to dash from his seat to the edge of the room and then move to the back, where the bathrooms were located.

The man's voice washed over him as he approached, not hearing a word. He was only focused on getting to Dante… who in that moment opened the bathroom door. But even though he was still a couple of dozen feet away, Oliver could see Brian was right behind him, saying something Oliver couldn't make out. He reached out to touch Dante's shoulder, causing Dante to spin around…

And push Brian back inside the bathroom.

Oliver stopped walking.

Did he really want to go in there? Would he be stopping a fight…or a fuck? Was this Brian and Dante's moment alone to work through their rage when everyone else was listening to the speeches?

Oliver didn't know how long they'd been together, but enough that Dante's mom had begun seriously planning a wedding. What did Oliver have on that? A couple of hours' conversation?

He should just leave them to it. He bit his lip and moved away from the wall where he'd stopped. A few people from the closest table were eying him up as if asking what the hell he was doing.

He had no idea.

Just as he started to move, however, a hand wrapped around his arm and began walking him faster. He snapped his head to see it was none other than Dante's mom, Francine.

"Oh, uh," Oliver sputtered as she marched them toward the lobby. "I'm so sorry. I was just going to get Dante—"

"Let them be," Francine snipped, releasing him once they were out of the main room. "I'm not sure what ridiculous stunt my son is pulling by inviting some millennial who thinks he's a peacock to his family's event, but I'm having none of it."

Oliver frowned, the wine making him a little bolder than usual. "You know Dante's a millennial as well, right?"

"Brian is *good* for him," Francine snapped. She smiled suddenly, and Oliver looked to see that she'd caught eyes with someone back in the room. She nodded and waved her fingers, then moved Oliver out of the line of sight of the door, dropping her cheery expression as fast as she'd pulled it up. "If Dante is going to be *different,* he needs to do it in the right way."

"By being miserable?" Oliver said, unable to stop himself. "By staying with someone who disrespects him and psychologically abuses him? Just because he has a fancy job?" He scoffed. "Lady, it's well into the twenty-first century. Being gay really isn't that different or scandalous."

Francine sniffed and folded her hands in front of her. "Quite frankly, Brian is none of your business, and *I* know what's best for my *son*. In case it was unclear, you are *not* the right way. The nerve of you to just show up here, uninvited—"

"Dante invited me, and that's all that matters," Oliver interrupted.

Except...it wasn't all that mattered. In all likelihood, Dante was in the bathroom with Brian right now, fucking. The realization made Oliver's heart want to crack, but he wouldn't give Francine the satisfaction of seeing him get upset.

"Excuse me," he said curtly. He didn't wait for a reply. He

just spun around and headed toward the door that would take him out the back. He had the need to go sit by the lake in the hopes that the water might take his troubles away.

He'd been having such a nice time.

He unbuttoned the top of his shirt and ambled sadly down toward one of the benches that looked out over the lake. The summer twilight lingered around him, and there was a stillness to the air that gave him a small bit of comfort.

This was always going to be a strange night, he reminded himself. Dante had walked into Aquarium mere hours ago, looking for someone to pretend to be his boyfriend. That wasn't exactly the start of a fairy tale. If it hadn't been for Emery and Kamran, Dante wouldn't have even considered Oliver, and Oliver wouldn't have been convinced to accept in return.

This was obviously doomed from the start. Hopefully, in a few weeks' time Oliver would be able to see the funny side of it, and maybe one day it would even be a silly story to tell his friends.

But…just for a little while, it had been nice to bask in Dante's attention and pretend this really had been a first date. That those sparks of electricity Oliver had felt between them had been real and could possibly even the start of something amazing.

Oliver pulled his phone out and toyed with it between his fingers as he watched the water gently lapping at the lake's shore. He took several slow, calming breaths, letting the waves soothe him. This really wasn't the end of the world. He'd had several dates far worse than this in his life.

But he'd never fallen for anyone of those guys like he had for Dante.

Which was crazy. You couldn't feel that strongly for someone so fast. Could you?

He looked down at his phone. He'd gotten it out with the

intention of messaging someone for a lift. He absolutely *could* afford an Uber, fuck you very much, Brian. But a childish part of him wanted to call his mom and ask her to pick him up.

No wonder Dante had chosen Brian over him. Why would he want to be with a young, insecure guy like him who hadn't even finished college when Brian was a big fancy finance guy who was probably an absolute jackhammer in bed?

Before he even registered what was happening, huge hands grabbed his shoulders and pulled him to his feet. Then Oliver was looking into the blazing eyes of Brian, and fear crashed through him bigger than any of the waves from the lake.

"I don't get it," Brian said, shaking his head and laughing dangerously. "What the fuck is Dante thinking?"

"Get *off* me!" Oliver cried.

He pushed against Brian's arms and wriggled to try and get out of his hands. But Brian dug his fingers in harder, and Oliver gasped.

"Maybe I should have a taste, hmm?" Brian growled, yanking Oliver's face closer. His sour whiskey breath made Oliver cough, and he struggled harder, genuinely afraid. "See, why the hell Dante would embarrass me like that? Over *you?* You're a child, and a ridiculous one at that!"

"At least I'm not a fucking psycho," Oliver spat. "Let me *go!*"

Dante's fist came flying out of nowhere, connecting with Brian's jaw and making him stagger backward, pinwheeling his arms. Oliver stumbled to his feet, his mouth hanging open as he watched Brian right himself. But then Dante's large hands were cradling Oliver's face with such tenderness, and Oliver found himself gazing into Dante's gorgeous brown eyes.

"Are you okay?" Dante asked urgently. "You weren't at the table, then I heard yelling through the door. I ran as fast as I could."

Oliver managed not to burst into tears, but only just. He threw his arms around Dante's back and pressed his head to his chest, inhaling deeply. "I'm fine. Thanks to you."

"Hey!" a woman's voice snapped.

Oliver opened his eyes and jerked his head just in time to see Jilly skid to a halt in front of them in her fancy dress, her Hermès clutch raised like a weapon as Brian tried to advance on Oliver and Dante, rubbing his jaw with a mulish expression.

"In case it wasn't clear before," Jilly hissed, brandishing the expensive clutch, "your invitation to this party – to this *family* – has been rescinded!"

"You heard the lady," said Dante darkly. He was stroking Oliver's back and keeping him pressed right against his chest. "I never want to see your face or even hear your name again, Brian. Leave now, and lose my number." He sneered. "And my mother's fucking number, you psycho."

Oliver couldn't help it. A small, slightly hysterical laugh bubbled out of him. "That's what *I* called him."

"You were right, sweetheart," Dante said softly.

The pet name made something beautiful and warm unfurl in Oliver's chest. Dante's expression was still harsh, though, as he glared at Brian. Brian looked between Oliver in Dante's arms and Jilly with her raised purse, then scoffed and shook his head.

"Like you're even worth all this bullshit." He rolled his eyes and stalked off, still fussing over his jaw where Dante had slugged him.

Just as he approached the entrance back into the country club, Francine came tottering out as fast as she could on her pumps. She waved her hands at Brian, shaking her head and smiling desperately. "Brian, darling! What's going on? I trust everything is all right? I…"

She trailed off as he stormed past her without speaking or even looking at her. Then her expression dropped as she looked at her children and Oliver. She began marching over, her finger wagging. But Dante was already walking toward her with Oliver pressed to his side, Jilly right behind them.

"Dante, you go and fix this right now," Francine snapped as they neared one another, but Dante shook his head.

"Good night, Mother. Jilly, please convey my warmest wishes to Rebecca and Louis. I promise to make this appalling display up to them with dinner soon." He beamed down at Oliver. "Maybe if my *boyfriend* forgives me, he might come, too. But right now, I need to take him out of here and make sure he's okay."

Oliver hardly heard Francine's indignant spluttering or Jilly's delighted squeal as Dante walked them past both the women back inside the lobby.

"Boyfriend?" Oliver whispered.

Dante gave him a one-armed shrug, not taking his eyes off him. "Maybe? If you'd like? Why don't I take you somewhere quiet where we can talk about it?"

Oliver tried to swallow the lump that had formed in his throat. He'd gone from happy to rejected to scared to treasured, all in the space of twenty minutes, and he was a little dizzy.

But he knew what his heart wanted.

"I'd love that," he whispered.

Dante smiled down at him, his eyes dancing over Oliver's face. Then he stopped walking as he gently cupped Oliver's jaw, brushing his thumb over his cheekbone before leaning down and pressing his lips to Oliver's.

Best. Date. Ever.

6

———

DANTE

Oliver tasted of red wine and sunshine. Dante's heart was still banging from the adrenaline of seeing Brian put his hands on Oliver. But at least now his racing pulse was less because of his fury and more because he finally had Oliver in his arms, just like he'd wanted for the past few hours.

Oliver melted into him, moaning as the kiss deepened. When Dante parted his lips and licked into Oliver's mouth, Oliver met him with his own tongue. Their hands gripped at each other's clothes and bodies as if they were clinging to driftwood in a storm. Oliver didn't need to worry, though. Dante wasn't letting him go.

"Come back to my place," Dante murmured.

Oliver blinked, his mouth hovering millimeters from Dante's, looking up into his eyes. For a moment, he seemed to consider. Then he smiled and nodded. "Yes."

Dante grinned, kissing his lips again, then took Oliver's hand and raised it to kiss his knuckles. He was almost giddy he was so happy. He'd been on a few dates since he'd broken up with Brian, but none of them had felt like this. It was as if

Dante was terrified of letting Oliver out of his sight, especially after the shit Brian had just pulled.

But it was more than that. Dante felt exhilarated in Oliver's company. Being with Brian had always been such hard work – a never-ending competition. Dante had only known Oliver a few hours, and yet he'd made Dante feel elevated, like he had a whole new outlook on life and could achieve anything.

He didn't want the night to end, but lucky for him, it didn't have to.

He led Oliver back outside into the warm summer's evening, already summoning a private car to whisk them away. Dante had an apartment rental for the weekend, and as he glanced behind them back into the empty lobby, he was even more grateful he'd made that decision. He'd had quite enough of his mother's interfering and was more than ready to get away from everyone so he could just have Oliver all to himself.

"You ended up shielding me in the end," Oliver commented. He still had his arms around Dante, so Dante's rubbed his back as he looked down at him.

"I don't know," Dante said. "I think having you here did exactly what I'd hoped. Why would I want anything to do with Brian when you're so amazing?"

Oliver blushed, the pink looking lovely under his teal-and-purple hair. "I thought…" He puffed out his cheeks and frowned but then apparently seemed to come to a decision from the way he nodded. "When I saw you push Brian back into the bathroom, I thought maybe you were going to have some of that infamous angry sex."

Dante practically choked. "What? Oh, hon. I'm so sorry you saw that. But I pushed him back in there because I just didn't want to make a scene while the speeches were going on. I swear. The thought of fucking him made me feel *ill.*"

"Oh," said Oliver, but his small smile showed how pleased he was.

Dante nuzzled his nose against Oliver's cheek and hair. "We don't have to do anything tonight if you don't want to. But the thought of being alone and naked with *you* makes me feel completely differently. Just so you know."

Oliver giggled and bit his lip before leaning up to kiss Dante again. "Duly noted," he said, his voice practically a purr.

The car arrived before they could get any further carried away, which was probably for the best. Dante's pants were already feeling tight. It wasn't a long drive back to the place he'd rented, and he contented himself by simply holding Oliver's hand for the journey, rubbing his knuckles with his thumb.

There was a kind of electricity between them as they took the elevator up to the fifth floor of the building, like the brewing of a summer storm. Dante held Oliver's hand as he led him into the apartment, giving Oliver a moment to look around appreciatively. Personally, Dante had a more rustic taste in home décor, but this sleek, modern place was a nice change for a vacation.

For a brief moment he wondered if he'd be able to bring Oliver to his home back in Seattle sometime soon, but that was getting ahead of himself. There was plenty of time to think about the future later. Right now, he wanted to treasure the moment.

This evening could have gone very differently. He was just so grateful that he'd seen Brian with his hands on Oliver and reached him in time before any real damage could have been done. After that fright, he wanted to make the most of his good fortune.

"Hey," he said softly as he wrapped his arms around Oliver, getting his full attention.

Oliver grinned. "Hey," he said back.

They leaned in together, finding each other's mouths again to kiss. It started soft and sensual, but then Dante's hands drifted up Oliver's back, holding him tighter, and heat rose within him. Oliver gripped his jacket lapels, his kisses hungry now as he pulled Dante to him. Dante moved one of his hands to card through Oliver's beautiful hair, tugging it and earning the most delicious moan from his throat. Dante kissed down his jaw and onto his neck, chasing the sound.

"Come to bed with me?" he asked. He'd promised himself he wouldn't move too fast or push Oliver, but he knew what he desperately wanted, and he'd be a fool if he didn't at least ask.

"Fuck, yes, Dante," Oliver uttered, pushing him toward the bedroom door. Dante laughed. So much for going too fast. Oliver seemed like he was just as eager as he was.

Dante hadn't even bothered unpacking when he'd checked in earlier. He'd been dead set on getting to Aquarium and scouting for someone to help him with his dilemma. He'd hoped he might find an okay date. He'd never dreamed he might meet someone who could be an *actual* boyfriend.

He was one lucky guy.

He shrugged off his jacket, not caring that the expensive garment crumpled to the floor. He'd get it dry-cleaned along with the rest of the suit. All that mattered now was being as close to Oliver as possible.

Between messy, smiling kisses, they began undressing themselves and each other, pushing far too many buttons through holes in their eagerness to get skin on skin. When they were down to their briefs, Dante dragged Oliver down onto the bed with him, groaning as their chests rubbed together and legs entwined.

Even through two layers of cotton, Dante could feel how

hot and hard Oliver's cock was. He was pretty big, and Dante couldn't wait to taste him. But for the moment they continued to kiss and frot, their bodies rolling together as their hands squeezed and caressed one another.

"You're so gorgeous," Dante murmured, trailing kisses along Oliver's chest. "My beautiful exotic bird."

Oliver giggled at that, then moaned deeply as Dante found one of his nipples to suck. Dante liked that Oliver's body was broad and felt strong, but he didn't have much in the way of muscle definition. His skin was soft and supple under Dante's hands as he explored his new lover. Now that they were nearly naked, Dante could see all of Oliver's colorful tattoos, and he couldn't wait to ask the stories behind all of them.

He was pretty sure he was going to get plenty of time to do so, a thought that filled him with contentment and joy to his bones.

Oliver pulled at Dante's hair, demanding his mouth to kiss again. An exhilarating thrill rushed through Dante. He wasn't fond of passive partners in bed, and if Oliver already felt confident enough to ask for what he wanted, that was a very good sign.

When Dante reached for Oliver's underwear, Oliver immediately helped him pull the briefs down before kicking them to the floor. Then they made short work of Dante's as well. Oliver dropped his head back and gasped as Dante wrapped his hand around both their cocks, rubbing them together. He kissed the long line of Oliver's exposed neck, then nipped his earlobe between his teeth.

"Dante," Oliver cried, digging his fingers into Dante's back. "Fuck, I want you. Want you inside me."

Dante slowed his hand and looked into Oliver's eyes. The dark blue was like the ocean, and they sparkled just like water. "Are you sure?" Dante wanted that as well, desperately, but he didn't usually fall into bed with a guy and fuck him on the first night.

However, there was nothing 'usual' about Oliver.

Oliver nodded. "Do you top?" he asked so sweetly. "I like both, but I'd really love to bottom for you tonight."

Dante was determined to stop thinking about Brian, even if it was to compare Oliver favorably to him. But it had always been such a battle with Brian to consider bottoming for Dante, who also liked to switch.

He shook his head and brushed Oliver's hair back from his forehead. "I'm starting to think you're perfect," he said with sincere warmth, then marveled at the beautiful blush that stained not just Oliver's cheeks but across his chest as well. "I like both, too. But I'd love to top you tonight."

He cupped the side of Oliver's face and kissed him tenderly for a moment, until Oliver began rolling his hips, rubbing their cocks together again as he moaned. Dante laughed at his enthusiasm. Wordlessly he nipped at Oliver's bottom lip, then moved off the bed to find his toiletry bag in his suitcase, thankful to his past self for having the foresight to pack condoms and lube.

When he turned back and saw Oliver on the bed, his arms above his head as he waited patiently for Dante to return, his cock red and leaking, Dante's breath caught. Had he said beautiful before? No, his exotic bird was fucking *stunning*.

He dropped back onto the bed and loomed over Oliver, his hands on either side of Oliver's head as he captured his mouth for a greedy, searing kiss. Oliver matched his fervor, scratching at Dante's shoulders as their tongues and teeth clashed. But Dante had promised to fuck Oliver, and his cock didn't want to wait too much longer to sink into this gorgeous man.

So Dante left the condoms beside them on the increasingly rumpled bed sheets and kept the lube in his hand as he kissed his way down Oliver's chest and stomach. Oliver bucked as Dante swallowed the tip of his cock, sucking hard and tonguing his slit as he squeezed and stroked the rest of his shaft. He tasted salty and musky, making Dante moan as he reveled in the first of what he hoped was many, *many* blow jobs to come.

He paused to pop the cap off the lube and squeeze some onto his fingers. Oliver hissed as the coldness touched his pucker, then moaned in pleasure as Dante began rubbing against his entrance. For a while, Dante just caressed him as he sucked his cock, but he wanted to make sure that Oliver was well stretched for him, so he pushed his middle finger inside up to the first knuckle, feeling how hot and tight Oliver was.

"Dante," Oliver rasped, his fingers tangled in Dante's hair as he pushed himself against Dante's finger, encouraging his finger farther inside. "Oh, yes, more."

Dante laughed around his cock, very much enjoying the demanding. For the next several minutes, he leisurely lapped and sucked at Oliver's cock until he had two fingers fully inside him. Then he kissed the tip one last time before licking and nuzzling his way past Oliver's heavy balls, kissing down to his stretched hole.

The sounds Oliver made as Dante began to eat him out were completely pornographic. Dante used his tongue to stretch his lover that last little bit, savoring his intimate, musky taste. Oliver was holding his own cheeks apart, so Dante reached between his own legs and took his half-hard cock in hand. It only took a few strokes to get himself hard as steel again. Then he picked up the condom packet.

Oliver watched him roll the condom down, panting and glistening with perspiration. He looked so delicious Dante had to kiss him on the mouth once he was done, climbing on top of him and lining up his cock with Oliver's prepared entrance. Still, there was always that resistance as he pushed through the ring of muscle, and Oliver cried out into Dante's mouth as he breached him.

Dante stilled, allowing Oliver a moment to get used to the intrusion. As Oliver breathed heavily and gripped Dante's shoulders, Dante placed sweet kisses over Oliver's cheeks, forehead, nose, and closed eyes.

"Are you okay?" he asked after a few moments.

Oliver exhaled and opened his eyes, nodding as he met Dante's gaze. "You feel amazing," he said, his voice raw. It tugged at Dante's heart, knowing he'd affected him like that.

"So do you," he told him truthfully.

Oliver rocked his hips, signaling he was ready for more, and Dante obliged by easing his way farther inside, kissing Oliver as they became as close as possible. When he bottomed out, Dante rested for a second, cradling Oliver to him, feeling his racing heartbeat.

"You're so beautiful," he said in the moment of quiet. "Inside and out."

Oliver hummed, kissing his shoulder and rubbing his back until their lips found each other again. The kisses were tender as Dante began to rock, thrusting inside his lover. Oliver dropped his head back and wailed as Dante found his prostate, and once he had the right angle, Dante started pistoning his hips to really drive Oliver wild. A part of him hoped there were neighbors around to hear them. He wanted the whole world to know he was claiming Oliver as his own.

Oliver clung to his neck as they slammed against one another, the air filled with the sounds of their skin slapping and their sawing breaths. Dante could feel himself peaking, so he reached down and began to jack Oliver off, his cock plenty slippery enough from where he'd been leaking precum.

Dante drank in the sight of him. "You're so fucking

beautiful," he gasped. "Come for me, baby. Come all over yourself."

Oliver screwed up his eyes and cried out, and within a few more strokes, he was spurting thick, white ropes all over his chest, painting his peachy skin and colorful tattoos. The sight of him coming undone tipped Dante over the edge, and he thrust one last time before he was emptying his balls into the condom buried within Oliver.

For the next few minutes, they lay side by side and clung to each other, Oliver's mess smeared between their chests as they floated down from their orgasms. When Dante had the strength, he gently kissed the side of Oliver's face and brushed his wet hair back.

"Holy fuck," Oliver said with a laugh. Then he blinked and turned his head so he could look Dante in the eye. "That was amazing."

"It was," Dante agreed with a grin. His heart was so full it was in danger of bursting.

They kissed a little longer until Oliver sighed. "We should probably clean up," he said regretfully.

Their cum was becoming a cold, sticky mess between them, and Dante had to admit it was unpleasant. He eased his way out of Oliver, pulling the condom from his shaft and tying off the end.

"Shower with me?" he asked.

Oliver nodded, kissing Dante again before they hauled themselves off the bed.

Dante took a moment to work out the unfamiliar shower dial, then hugged Oliver to him as the water heated up. "Will you stay the night?"

For a moment, Oliver considered him before sighing happily. "I'll stay as long as you want me," he said, resting the side of his head on Dante's chest.

Dante stroked his damp hair, unable to stop himself from

grinning. "That might be a very long time," he said with a hum.

"Good," said Oliver against his skin.

Dante had walked into a bar earlier that day, looking for some help. He'd never imagined he'd walk out again with the chance to fall in love, but he had a strong suspicion as he cradled Oliver in the steamy bathroom that was exactly what he'd gotten.

EPILOGUE

Oliver – Six Months Later

OLIVER BREATHED IN DEEPLY AS HE STROLLED DOWN PINE Cove's main street, heading toward the boardwalk. Christmas lights twinkled from all directions, and the air was filled with festive music and the sounds of happy voices. He smiled, his face tingling in a pleasant way against the cold.

How much could change in half a year.

He and Dante would soon be joining their friends at Aquarium, but Oliver had told his boyfriend he'd meet him down by the lake on their favorite bench. They had a favorite bench now. They had a *lot* of things together as a couple.

When Dante had said Oliver could stay as long as he wanted after their first night together, he'd really meant it. They'd needed to vacate the rental apartment the next morning and had spent all their time either sleeping or making love until they'd had to leave. But then Dante had taken Oliver out for brunch at Sunny Side Up that had lasted for hours, then they'd gone for a walk around the lake, ending up sitting at the very bench where Oliver was heading to now.

It was there Dante had officially asked Oliver to be his boyfriend. He'd had to head back to Seattle that evening, but he did so with a promise they would make the blossoming thing between them work.

And they had.

It had been long distance for a while, and that brought some difficulties with it, especially with Oliver having to work so many weekends at the bar. But back in September, he'd decided to go back to his former community college and was now only working a couple of weeknight shifts at Aquarium while he was focusing on finishing his degree.

That meant he'd been able to spend most weekends in Seattle, which they'd preferred because Dante had been renting his own place, and neither of them wanted to impose on Oliver's parents.

But all that had changed last month, when Dante had finally quit his job at the big real estate company and found a place right here in town and invited Oliver to move in with him.

Oliver bit his lip as the familiar warm burst of pride filled him that he'd finally moved out and had his own home now. He was mostly just contributing to the bills at the moment, as his income from the bar had dropped dramatically and Dante insisted that was only fair while he was studying. But he'd also said that perhaps they could buy their next place together.

Their *next* place. *Buy.*

Oliver marveled at how much faith Dante had in their future. Everything just seemed so easy with him. Like he knew no matter what, things would work out okay. This wasn't the longest relationship Oliver had ever been in, but it felt by far the strongest to him, and he had to agree that it was easy to see it lasting a very long time.

Maybe even forever.

He was pleased to see as he wandered past the boardwalk down to the lake that their special bench was unoccupied. The dark winter's night was illuminated by the street lighting and fairy lights wrapped around the posts, so Oliver could still see the waves lapping at the shore as he sat down.

The breeze was cold and bracing off the water, but he had a lot of layers on, and his gloved hands were stuffed in his coat pockets. So he simply enjoyed the view as he waited for Dante to come meet him, letting the wind whip around him. It felt cleansing.

He could have gone to Aquarium and met up with his friends. He loved that he got to hang out with them on the other side of the bar more often than not these days. But he was still not over the fact that Dante was living in Pine Cove now and they could see each other all the time. His friends teased him about being in the honeymoon phase of their relationship still, but Oliver didn't care. Actually, he loved it.

He was one of those big saps now who made goo-goo eyes at his man, and he didn't care who knew it.

Dante had chosen *him.* He'd seen how special Oliver was when Oliver hadn't even seen it himself. And he'd specifically chosen Oliver over that douchebag Brian and the wishes of Dante's own mother.

Oliver sighed, filled with bittersweet thoughts. Brian had mercifully not darkened their doorstep since the infamous party, but they'd heard through Jilly that several allegations of sexual assault had come out against him at his job, and he'd been fired. So much for how impressive he looked on paper now.

That was the good news. The bad news was that Francine

was still being ridiculous, insisting that Dante had thrown away a perfect husband, even after news of the allegations had come to light. She was the only one defending Brian, and Dante was having none of it.

So next week, Oliver and Dante were visiting Jilly for an early holiday celebration, but then they were spending actual Christmas here in Pine Cove as a couple and visiting Oliver's family. It hurt Oliver's heart that Dante's mother would choose her stubborn pride over her son, but maybe this would make her come to her senses, and next year would be better.

Oliver wasn't sure she'd ever approve of him, but he had Dante's unwavering support, and that was all that mattered. Plus, Oliver's parents absolutely *adored* Dante. His mom was always baking him something, and his dad liked to get him around to tinker with the lawn mower together or some other outdoorsy gadgetry thing. Oliver loved it.

Oliver would just have to make sure that Dante had the most amazing holiday season, and that was starting tonight with their friends' celebration on the town. They were all wearing ugly Christmas sweaters and were planning on drinks to start, as much Chinese food as they could manage to eat, and then probably some truly appalling karaoke.

Oliver couldn't wait.

Actually, they'd had their first Christmas party the week before with their new rock-climbing club. Oliver loved that they were making new friends together as a couple, and since Dante had moved into town permanently, they'd been able to commit to officially joining the club.

One of their friends, Elias, was Jewish and estranged from his unaccepting family, so he and his newly wed husband, Ben, were hosting a big Hanukkah party. They were also going back to Seattle to meet up with Dante's friends at a big house party. Oliver was pleased to say that he really liked the group and had been accepted with open arms and more than one "You're *so* much better than Brian," which he reveled in. And then of course there was Sunny and Tyee's infamous family New Year's Eve bash, which Oliver was honored that he and Dante had been invited to this year.

He rubbed his eyes for a second, blaming the wind and glad no one could see him. But he allowed himself a little moment to cherish the fact that family wasn't just the people you were related to. It was also friends, and it turned out he and Dante had an abundance of those. Family came in all forms, including the small family he and Dante were starting.

They'd both gotten each other a ridiculous amount of presents in their excitement of their first Christmas together. Dante had promised not to spend too much so Oliver wouldn't feel outdone, but Oliver had handmade a few things that he hoped would have way more sentimental value than anything he could have bought.

However, something they'd decided to get together for each other was their very own puppy. In the new year, they were going to the shelter to adopt because unfortunately, they knew there were bound to be unwanted Christmas pets to rescue. Oliver loved the idea of giving a dog that had gotten off to a bad start a forever home where they would be loved and cherished for the rest of their lives.

He was so lost in his daydream that he startled when someone sat down next to him. But luckily it was Dante, as expected. Oliver smiled happily at him as he pulled him in for a big squishy hug through their coats and sweaters.

"Hey, babe," Oliver said excitedly. "How did it go?"

Dante kissed him, his grin telling it all. "All done," he said with a sigh. "I'll officially be opening my own business in the new year. The lease is signed, and the place is mine."

Oliver squealed and grabbed Dante's face to kiss him again with more enthusiasm. The holidays were a strange time to try and start a business, but Dante had been working toward this for months – almost since he'd met Oliver. It was as if the moment the seed had been planted that he absolutely could start his own small real estate business, he'd been on a mission.

At first, Oliver had been a bit apprehensive that Dante wanted to commit to Pine Cove so soon. Because that also meant committing to Oliver, and that felt like such a huge step. But Dante had been so calm about it. He'd known what he'd wanted and gone for it until Oliver had been helpless but to accept that this brilliant, handsome man was all in when it came to the two of them.

"It's the start of a new era," he said happily, snuggling up to Dante's side so they could both watch the waves lapping at the shore. Despite the wind, the water looked calm and assured. Just like Oliver felt.

"It's the beginning of the rest of our lives," Dante said, making Oliver's insides all warm and tingly. "New home, new careers, all with my man by my side."

"Damn right," Oliver agreed.

He still wasn't sure what kind of career he wanted, but he had time to think about that, especially with Dante's unwavering support. For now, they had moved in together, were meeting each other's friends and making new ones, adopting a dog, and Dante had even suggested that he wanted to take them to Japan for a proper vacation next year. Oliver had suggested they wait for things to settle down a bit before booking anything like that, just to make sure they weren't doing too much too fast. But secretly, he knew he would absolutely love to go on his dream trip with Dante.

They watched the lake for a little longer, then decided to go meet their friends. They headed up the boardwalk hand in hand, enjoying the festive decorations in comfortable quietness. That was shattered as they made their way into

Aquarium, where the crowd was already in full party mode to the loud pop music playing over the sound system.

Their friends were easy to spot in the couple of booths they'd reserved. There were so many of them now that they were all loved up with their partners. Oliver laughed as Emery spotted them and yelled, waving his hands as he and several of the others called them over.

"I'll get us some drinks," Dante said with a laugh and kissed Oliver's cheek. "What would you like?"

"Hmm," said Oliver, pretending to think. "I guess they're all out of boyfriends?"

Dante rolled his eyes and laughed because Oliver liked to make this joke a lot. But then his gaze became sultry, and he wrapped his arms around Oliver's back, nuzzling their noses together. "They're fresh out of boyfriends. I checked. But they might have a husband for you."

Oliver's jaw dropped. "R-really?" he squeaked.

Dante looked far too pleased with himself for shocking Oliver like that. "Yup. Not today, though. But one day. Maybe."

Oliver breathed again. For a second, he'd thought Dante was actually proposing, and as much as he loved him, Oliver wasn't sure he was ready for another big commitment so soon.

But 'maybe one day soon' he liked the sound of. He liked the sound of that a *lot*.

"One day," he said as the grin spread across his face. He leaned up to kiss the man of his dreams, wondering how he got so lucky in life.

This was just the beginning, that was for sure.

The beginning of forever.

FRESH SNOW

ABOUT THIS STORY

Emery Klein is throwing the best Christmas party ever, but his fiancé, Scout Duffy, and all their friends have something more exciting in mind.

Fresh Snow is a follow up to Pine Cove #2: Troubles Waters, set after #6: Thin Ice. It is also the final story in the Pine Cove series. 4.1K words.

1

EMERY

"Oh em *gee*, it's really starting to feel like Christmas!"

Emery Klein clasped his hands together, spinning around as he admired all the hard work everyone had put in so far to make The Peaks Country Club look like a true winter wonderland.

The friendship group he considered his family had decided to throw a huge bash this year, and of course Emery had taken the lead with the party planning. Nobody knew how to celebrate like he did, after all.

He'd been working over every detail for the past few months, and finally the day was here. He'd been up since the crack of dawn, fueled at first by copious amounts of coffee, but now that the work was almost complete, he was sipping on his first glass of Champagne, feeling a deep sense of satisfaction.

He was so blessed. He got along well enough with his mom and dad, but it was these friends here that made Pine Cove feel like home. Not to mention a certain hotter-than-hell boxing coach who had saved his life and stolen his heart a few years ago.

Emery smiled to himself, warmth overflowing from his heart as he admired the engagement ring on his left hand. One day, he would plan the most perfect wedding for him and Scout there ever was. But right now, he had Christmas to see through.

There were several round tables set up with chrysanthemums, tea lights in little glass jars, holly sprigs, and cinnamon sticks. He'd even added a little spray of fake snow to each display, just to give it that extra special Christmassy touch. It hadn't snowed for real in Pine Cove yet, even though Emery kept hoping it would. That would just be the icing on the cake for their festivities.

All around the room were fresh pine trees. As the town's name suggested, Pine Cove had a thriving Christmas tree industry, and the country club always had several enormous ones set up in their function rooms and in the lobby. Before planning his color scheme, Emery had coordinated with their events team so his party could match. There were teal and silver baubles everywhere, as well as huge red bows.

Emery sighed, straightening up one of the nearby candy canes that were placed on every plate. The staff was still rushing around, adding all the little finishing touches to the tables. There was also a stage where the town's children's choir was going to be performing later. Emery grinned to himself, thinking of his friends Swift and Micha's little girl. Imogen couldn't carry a tune in a bucket, but she'd learned every single word to her solo in ASL so Micha's deaf niece could understand what she was singing.

This was what Christmas was about. Family. Connectedness. Emery couldn't wait for everyone to arrive. And it wasn't just his immediate friendship group that he was catering for tonight. The invites had gone out to everyone's families as well, especially the huge broods of the Coals and the Perkinses. Some of his friend Ben Turner's distant relations and their friends were coming all the way from England to spend the holidays here in the Pacific Northwest.

It was going to be an incredibly special day.

This was one of the reasons Emery worked so hard the rest of the year. Being a reasonably famous and ridiculously well-paid influencer was kind of lonely in the old days. But now that he had so many nearest and dearest to spoil all the time, nothing brought him more joy.

"Wow," a voice came by his ear, making him jump. "You really went all out, didn't you?"

Guests weren't supposed to arrive for another half an hour or so, but it didn't surprise Emery that one of his best friends, Robin Coal, was a little early. He was a very organized sort of guy. His red hair shone in the light of a thousand Christmas lights, his delight clear to see.

Emery hummed and spun around, beaming. He'd gone for a Billy Porter look, with a classic black tux and white shirt on his top half, complemented by an enormous layered black skirt and black heeled boots hidden underneath. He felt super glamorous. Perfect as the hostess with the mostest.

"She tries," he said, feigning modesty, touching his chest, and sighing.

Robin nudged Emery in his ribs with his elbow and raised his eyebrow. "How can you pull all this together in a few weeks, and yet you still haven't set a date for your wedding?"

Emery bit his lip, feeling that familiar anxiety rise within him. "You know why," he told Robin quietly. "Scout is *perfect*. His proposal was *perfect*. I just have to figure out how I can possibly show what he means to me in only one day. I don't know if we should go somewhere exotic or stay here or jump out of a *plane*. I just know it has to be amazing." He shook off his worries and grinned at his friend. "Maybe next year, I'll finally figure it out. But for now, it's Christmas!"

He linked arms with Robin and whisked him around in a circle, making Robin drop his head back and laugh. "It is certainly Christmas," he agreed. "The first one with our little turtle dove."

He finished the spin with Emery so they were now facing the back of the hall where Robin's muscular, tattooed, ex-Marine husband, Dair, was sitting at one of the tables. He was bouncing their newly adopted baby daughter, Dove, on his knee, pure love written all over his face.

Emery glanced over to see Robin looking at them both with such adoration it made Emery's heart skip a beat. "Being parents suits you both," Emery said sincerely. He knew the adoption process hadn't been easy for the couple, as these things rarely were, but he was certain it was going to be so worth it. That little girl was going to be loved silly.

Robin and Scout had only had a small, simple wedding earlier that year. Their priority had always been adopting a child, not to mention their menagerie of rescued pets. They were a very loving pair, and Emery was proud to call them his friends.

"Thanks, hon," Robin said. He kissed Emery's cheek, then made his way over to his husband and daughter, grinning and waving at the happy little baby.

Over the next several minutes, Emery made himself busy assisting the staff finishing all the final little details, sipping his Champagne merrily as he basked in his success. Everyone was going to have a wonderful time, he was certain.

There were a couple of his friends, like Kamran Amir and Elias Solomon, who were estranged from their families. Emery might not have much in common with his parents, but at least he still knew they loved him in their own way. As he looked over at baby Dove, he couldn't fathom how someone could disown a child simply for who they loved.

Even though Elias was Jewish, he still loved joining in with Christmas celebrations, and always threw a delightful Hanukkah party for all of them each year. Emery adored how they looked after each other and made sure no one felt alone or left out. That was one of the reasons all the presents under the tree today would not be for anyone here but would go to charitable causes so that children less fortunate than Dove would have something to open on Christmas Day.

It wasn't long before the room started filling up, and Emery was dashing around, ensuring he said hello to everyone. Wow, they'd all really gone all out on the glad rags, that was for sure. Fancy dresses and suits and everything in between were being sported by his festive guests. Good. Emery loved it when people understood the assignment.

Servers were handing out drinks, and most people were mingling rather than sitting, so there was quite a throng in the main hall now. That was probably how Emery missed being snuck up on.

"Is that mistletoe I see, or are you just happy to see me?"

Emery gasped and spun around, squeaking when he realized his fiancé, Scout, was now right in front of him, holding up a sprig of mistletoe above their heads.

Emery put his empty glass down and placed a finger on his chin, pretending to think. "Both," he said, unable to stop himself from grinning. "Can it be both?"

"Of course, gorgeous."

Scout leaned down and claimed Emery's mouth with a searing kiss. He gripped Emery's back with his free hand, digging his blunt fingers through Emery's clothes, making Emery's heart race. Just as things were getting a little NSFW, Scout pulled back and hummed.

"Merry Christmas, Emmerich."

For some strange reason, nerves fluttered through Emery's chest. Scout almost never called him by his full name, but he loved it when he did. It made him feel treasured.

"Merry Christmas, Scout," he replied, wishing his fiancé had a longer name so he could mimic the gesture. But from his smug, happy expression, Scout was already feeling pretty good.

"C'mere," he murmured, lacing his fingers with Emery's and tugging him away.

"Oh, but…" Emery tried to protest.

Scout knew him all too well, though. "Babe," he said patiently, bringing Emery's hand up to kiss the back of it. "Everything is perfect. The staff has it all in hand. You need to have fun tonight as well."

"No, I—"

"No means 'yes,' remember?" Scout interrupted him with a grin, repeating their favorite teasing mantra.

Emery whimpered and tried to find a way to argue against his fiancé's words of wisdom, but he was right, really. Also, Scout was super fucking hot and had that look in his eyes as he dragged Emery out of the room. Like a caveman who'd found his mate and wanted his way with him.

"Okay, I guess," Emery said, trying to sound pouty but not really succeeding. He winked at his fiancé and allowed himself to be manhandled.

"You look so fucking gorgeous," Scout growled. "Not just because of the clothes. You look so happy when you're looking after other people."

Emery smiled and went to say thank you, but suddenly Scout yanked him determinedly down a corridor. He pulled Emery into a linen closet, shutting the door firmly behind them. Emery squeaked, and his eyes went wide. Were they really doing this? They'd had sex in all kinds of places, so it wasn't that he was shy. But this was a big day, and he had to make sure everything went smoothly, and that people were having a good time, and—

"Ohhh," he moaned as Scout managed to get his hand up Emery's voluminous skirt to grope his cock at the same time he kissed Emery's neck. He fondled Emery through his tight thong, caressing his thickening dick and stroking his bare ass.

"I think you need a little distraction to relax you," Scout murmured against Emery's throat.

Despite going from zero to sixty on the arousal meter, Emery had to laugh. "There's nothing *little* about you," he said as he finally got with the program and gripped Scout's shoulders tightly through his fancy suit. Emery had to admit that his man looked *hot* in all his finery. They should do black tie more often.

"Damn right," Scout rumbled into his ear as he fished his hand down Emery's underwear to get his hand on his erection. Emery gasped and shuddered against him as he stroked him hard.

"I hate to be a party pooper," Emery whispered between whimpers, "but I don't want to make a mess of my pretty outfit."

Scout chuckled and kissed his mouth possessively.

"Don't worry, baby," Scout said, dropping to his knees. "I got you covered."

There was something crazy erotic about watching his big fiancé disappear underneath Emery's skirts. The fact that Emery couldn't see when Scout swallowed his length whole somehow made it more exciting.

"Shit, fuck, yes," Emery hissed as he grabbed onto a stack of neatly folded bedsheets behind him for support. "Like that, baby. Oh, fuck. So good."

He honestly hadn't realized how tense he'd been, but

Scout's mouth was soon draining all that stress right out of his cock. Emery moaned and panted, not really caring if anyone heard them. He sort of wanted people to know that his man was so desperate to have him that he just couldn't help but drag him into a closet to have his way with him.

Scout was talented with his mouth and knew exactly how to tease Emery for ages. But right now, he was hungry and frantic, drawing Emery's climax out of him fast, just like he needed. Not wanting to mess up Scout's hair (Emery had spent a good ten minutes styling it), he grabbed hold of Scout's shoulders through the skirt instead, helping to keep him standing as his knees began to give way.

"Scout, *fuck!*" Emery shouted. Anyone walking past their closet just then would have *definitely* heard that. But Emery was too busy shooting cum down his sexy-as-fuck fiancé's throat to care.

Emery trembled as his orgasm washed through him. Scout sucked him gently as he began to soften, then carefully tucked him away in his thong again before emerging from under the skirt. Scout was slightly red faced and a little sweaty. The closet certainly had a more masculine musk to it now, which added to Emery's post-bliss high.

"C'mere," he demanded, dragging Scout up for a filthy kiss. They crashed together in a passionate embrace, Emery getting lip gloss all over Scout's mouth and chin. Whatever. He could clean him off before they rejoined the party. Right now, Emery felt like marking him.

Too soon, though, Scout was pulling away. "All right. You feel ready to go face the music, now?" he asked.

Emery blinked at him in confusion. "What? No! You still have a not-so-little problem!"

He cupped Scout between his legs, feeling his rock-hard erection. Scout groaned and shook his head. "No, we haven't got time. I just wanted to help relax you, that's all."

Emery smirked and dropped to his knees, already attacking Scout's zipper. "No means 'yes,' remember?" he said, mimicking Scout's words back at him from earlier. "If you think I'm going to let my man go unsatisfied, you don't know me at all, Mr. Duffy. Besides, it's *my* party. I'll be a little late if I want to."

There were no more protests as Emery freed Scout's gorgeous cock and immediately devoured it whole. Scout gnashed his teeth and gripped Emery's shoulders, and Emery felt a pang of even deeper love for his fiancé.

Even amid the throes of passion, his man knew not to fuck with Emery's hair, just like Emery had done for him. If that wasn't true love, he wasn't sure what was.

WHEN THEY CREPT BACK out into the corridor a little while later, neatened up with a couple of mints in their mouths, Emery couldn't stop grinning. Every day was still an adventure with the gorgeous man he'd been so lucky to fall in love with.

Emery paused to make sure he'd gotten every smear of lip gloss off Scout's mouth. He thought about re-applying it to himself, but then he figured he was probably going to be making out with Scout for most of the evening anyway, so why bother. But as he double-checked his appearance in the reflection of the closest darkened window, he realized something.

"Snow," he said softly and with more than a little reverence.

It had started to feel like it would never come to Pine Cove, and yet as he approached the glass and peered out into the dark evening, there it was. It must have started falling not long after the guests started arriving and Emery stopped paying attention to the weather outside. There was already a thick, gleaming layer covering the ground and trees. Emery smiled to himself, looking out over the choppy waters of the lake beyond the country club's dock, seeing the delicate flakes vanishing into its depths.

It was beautiful but fleeting. You had to appreciate it in the moment before it was gone.

"Is there anything quite so perfect as fresh snow?" he murmured as Scout slipped his arms around his waist, hugging him from behind.

"You," Scout said with a hum, then kissed the side of Emery's neck, making him shiver.

Emery turned, his heart so full with love as he found Scout's mouth to kiss him with zeal. See – he knew it was a good idea not to put any more lip gloss on. His man was far too hot and romantic. Emery was powerless to his wiles.

"Oh, hey. There you are," a voice rang out before they could get too hot and heavy again. Emery extracted himself from Scout and looked down the corridor to see one of their best friends, Kamran, and his fiancé, Lee Marshall, striding toward them.

Emery tried not to blush, but he wasn't sure he succeeded. "Oh, um, were you looking for me? Is everything okay?" He checked his watch. Dinner wasn't due to be served for another hour. They were still on drinks and canapés. However, he was about to launch into panic mode regardless.

But Kamran waved his hands with a big smile, knowing Emery all too well. "Everything's fine, buddy. We just wanted to come say happy holidays."

He winked at Scout, who gave him a little scowl and shook his head. Emery was going to ask what that was about when Lee scooped him up in a hug. "Merry Christmas! Happy holidays!" he cried. Lee was one of their friends who had a huge family and would be spending the twenty-fifth with them (and Kamran, of course). Emery was glad that they could hold this party a week earlier so that everyone could get involved.

"Shall we make our way back to the main hall?" Kamran suggested.

There was a mischievous air about him as the four of them began walking, each couple hand in hand, and Emery rolled his eyes. He'd bet money they were up to something, but he trusted none of their friends would ever do anything malicious. So he resigned himself to being surprised. Perhaps someone had dressed up as Santa? That would be super cute.

"Oh, hey, Padilla," Lee called as they turned into the next corridor and saw Lee's colleague from the police station. Detective Padilla was still in one of her regular pantsuits, but she'd swapped her usual vat of coffee for a glass of Champagne and was talking to one of the English guests. Anika was some distant cousin of Ben's and was looking absolutely stunning in a red-and-gold sari.

Padilla almost dropped her glass and spluttered as she looked guiltily at Anika. "Hey, fellas," she said with an awkward wave. "We were just, um, you know-"

Anika rolled her eyes and grabbed Padilla's elbow. "We'll see you in the main hall," she said in her posh English accent. Then she winked at them before dragging the blushing detective along with her.

Emery chuckled. He hadn't known Padilla was into women, but he thought it was pretty adorable that she'd been embarrassed at getting caught flirting with Anika. If she only knew what he and Scout had just been up to.

"I think we should join them," Kamran said with a grin, whisking Lee after the two women.

Emery was about to follow when Scout took his hand, and Emery found himself looking into his wide green eyes.

Scout took a deep breath, bit his lip, then nodded. "I've got a surprise for you, baby," he murmured. "I hope you like it."

Emery frowned and gave a nervous chuckle. "Does this have anything to do with Kamran's not-so-subtle hints?" he asked.

Scout just hummed, though, then cupped the side of his face. "I love you, gorgeous," he said.

Okay. *Now* Emery was nervous.

"What's going on?" he asked as Scout led him back down the corridor. The place was eerily quiet. Had the sound system cut out? What was happening with the party? "Scout?"

Finally, Scout grinned. He was nervous as well, Emery was certain, but seeing him smile meant this couldn't be a bad thing, surely?

They stopped in front of the double doors, where Scout squeezed Emery's hands tightly. "Your friends and I decided you needed a little push. Otherwise it was never going to happen. I don't need perfect. I just need *you.*"

Before Emery could work out what that meant, Scout knocked on the door. What on earth? Why wouldn't he just open the door like a regular person?

Music stirred in the room beyond. Hang on…was that the children's choir? They weren't supposed to be on until later.

The doors suddenly swung inward, revealing all the party guests standing behind their allocated chairs…and some people Emery hadn't known were coming at all. "Mom? Dad?" he said as they came toward him and Scout.

"We wouldn't miss this for the world," his mother said, cupping his face and kissing both his cheeks. His dad clapped his shoulder and gave him a good squeeze.

Was the world ending? What the hell was going on?

That was when Emery realized the tables had been moved slightly. Instead of being evenly spread like they had been when he'd left the room, there was now a central aisle running from the door to the stage. It was covered in rose petals. And standing at the end was someone very official looking.

Realization hit Emery like a snowball, and he slapped his hand over his mouth as he gasped, tears springing in his eyes. "Scout," he whispered, hardly daring to believe it. "Are we getting married?"

He turned to look at his fiancé's hopeful face. "If you want to?" Scout whispered back. Emery was aware that everyone was looking at them, but all he cared about in that moment was Scout. "You seemed paralyzed trying to make it perfect. But *you're* perfect. Everything else is just gravy." He jutted his chin at their audience. "All the people we love are here, ready to party. What do you say?"

Emery looked out over the room. He'd had so many ideas...*too* many ideas. Scout was right. He'd been delaying and delaying because he wanted it to be flawless and spectacular. But really, what was more spectacular than this? Their friends were all obviously in on it from their gleeful faces. The children's choir was singing "Perfect" by Ed Sheeran, something Emery hadn't known they'd been practicing. But little Imogen Coal was there, signing and singing her heart out.

That was his and Scout's song. Of course it was because that was what Scout was to him. Perfect. The kids had obviously learned it especially for them, probably thanks to their teacher, Jay Coal, Robin's twin and one of Emery's other good friends.

Scout had gotten him out of the room so more of his friends could move the tables and scatter the rose petals. Kamran appeared at their sides, opening a small box to show two platinum wedding bands, presumably as he was Scout's best man. Speaking of which, Ava Coal strode up to Emery's side and slapped his back. If anyone was going to be his best man, it would be her.

"You're not going to fuck up all our hard work, are you?" she asked with a grin and a raised eyebrow. Mutely, Emery shook his head.

His friends – his *family* – had organized all this for him, to save him from himself. What could be more perfect than that? Because what made something truly incredible, he was realizing, was when it was exactly right and yet imperfect. Nothing in life was truly flawless. All that mattered was that you tried your best for the ones you loved.

In that moment, Emery felt loved by the whole wide world.

But mostly by Scout.

He turned to his fiancé, tears in his eyes as he nodded. "I'm ready. I love it. Let's get married, baby."

Because he didn't need the perfect wedding (although he had a feeling this was going to be pretty damn close). This was just one day. What was going to be perfect was all the days after this he'd get to spend with his husband, here in Pine Cove, with their crazy assortment of friends and families.

This was where he belonged – where they all belonged – and he wouldn't have it any other way.

ACKNOWLEDGMENTS

Cover - Cate Ashwood
Beta Reader - Amy Pittel
Editing - Meg Cooper
Proofing - Tanja Ongkiehong

ABOUT THE AUTHOR

HJ Welch is a contemporary MM romance author living in London with her husband and two balls of fluff that occasionally pretend to be cats. She began writing at an early age, later honing her craft online in the world of fanfiction on sites like Wattpad. Fifteen years and over a million words later, she sought out original MM novels to read. By the end of 2016 she had written her first book of her own, and in 2017 she fulfilled her lifelong dream of becoming a fulltime author. Her pronouns are she/they.

She also writes contemporary British MM romance as Helen Juliet.

You can contact HJ Welch via social media:

Website – http://www.hjwelch.com/

Newsletter – https://www.subscribepage.com/helenjuliet

Facebook Group – Helen's Jewels

Facebook Page – @HJWelchAuthor

Instagram – @helenjwrites

Twitter – @helenjwrites

Email – helenjulietauthor@gmail.com

www.ingramcontent.com/pod-product-compliance
Lightning Source LLC
Chambersburg PA
CBHW051228210726
48290CB00003B/855